"Empty and peaceful the old house dreamed, with sunlight shifting from room to room and no sound to break the silence, save in one place, where the voices of children could be heard faintly above the rustling of a tree."

—from "A Room Full of Leaves"
by Joan Aiken

PETER A. BARRETT teaches fourth- and sixth-grade classes at St. Albans School in Washington, D.C. He received a B.A. degree in English from Trinity College in Hartford, Connecticut, and a M.A. degree in teaching from Northwestern University. Mr. Barrett lives in Washington, D.C., with his wife and daughter.

TO BREAK THE SILENCE:

THIRTEEN SHORT STORIES FOR YOUNG READERS

JOAN AIKEN
KEVIN CROSSLEY-HOLLAND
WALTER D. EDMONDS
HOWARD M. FAST
LANGSTON HUGHES
SHIRLEY JACKSON
E. L. KONIGSBURG
PENELOPE LIVELY
NICHOLASA MOHR
KATHERINE PATERSON
PHILIPPA PEARCE
K. M. PEYTON
JILL PATON WALSH

EDITED BY PETER A. BARRETT

CHAPTER II

Published by
Dell Publishing Co., Inc.
1 Dag Hammarskjold Plaza
New York, New York 10017

Laurel-Leaf Library ® TM 766734, Dell Publishing Co., Inc.

ISBN: 0-440-98807-1

RL: 6.2

Printed in the United States of America

March 1986

10 9 8 7 6 5 4 3 2

WFH

Grateful acknowledgment is made for permission to reprint the following stories:

"The Tree in the Meadow" from *What the Neighbors Did and Other Stories* by Philippa Pearce. (Thomas Y. Crowell). Copyright © 1972 by Philippa Pearce. By permission of Harper & Row, Publishers, Inc. Published in England by Puffin Books (1975). Copyright © Philippa Pearce 1959, 1967, 1969, 1972. Reprinted by permission of Penguin Books Ltd.

"Water Never Hurt a Man" from *Mostly Canallers* by Walter D. Edmonds. Reprinted by permission of Harold Ober Associates Incorporated. Copyright 1930, 1958 by Walter D. Edmonds.

"On Shark's Tooth Beach" in *Throwing Shadows* by E. L. Konigsburg. Copyright © 1979 by E. L. Konigsburg. Reprinted with the permission of Atheneum Publishers.

"Thank You, Ma'am" from *The Langston Hughes Reader* by Langston Hughes. Reprinted by permission of Harold Ober Associates Incorporated. Copyright © 1958 by Langston Hughes.

"Woodrow Kennington Works Practically a Miracle" from *Angels and Other Strangers* by Katherine Paterson. (Thomas Y. Crowell). Copyright © 1979 by Katherine Paterson. Reprinted by permission of Harper & Row, Publishers, Inc. This story also appears in *Star of Night* by Katherine Paterson published in England by Victor Gollancz Ltd.

"Crossing to Salamis" from *Children of the Fox* by Jill Paton Walsh. Copyright © 1977, 1978 by Jill Paton Walsh. Reprinted by permission of Farrar, Straus and Giroux, Inc.

"A Man and a Boy" by K. M. Peyton. By permission of the author.

"Charles" from *The Lottery and Other Stories* by Shirley Jackson. Copyright 1948, 1949 by Shirley Jackson. Copyright renewed © 1976, 1977 by Laurence Hyman, Barry Hyman, Mrs. Sarah Webster and Mrs. Joanne Schnurer. Reprinted by arrangement with Farrar, Straus and Giroux, Inc.

"The Horseman" by Kevin Crossley-Holland from *Wordhoard* by Kevin Crossley-Holland and Jill Paton Walsh. By permission of Macmillan, London and Basingstoke.

"The Picnic" by Penelope Lively from *Young Winter Tales 6* edited by M. R. Hodgkin. Copyright Penelope Lively © 1975. First published by Macmillan & Co. Limited, London.

"A Very Special Pet" from *El Bronx Remembered: A Novella and Stories* by Nicholasa Mohr. Copyright © 1975 by Nicholasa Mohr. By permission of Harper & Row, Publishers, Inc.

For Katherines
Epes and Ashe

Contents

CHAPTER II

Philippa Pearce, "The Tree in the Meadow"

What sits outside your bedroom window—open fields, a backyard with patio and long-ignored swing set, or maybe a parking lot? For young Ricky it is and has always been a meadow dominated by a huge elm. Then that elm begins to lose its branches, reminding neighbors of its presence, its age, and, some think, its dangers. When Ricky learns of plans to fell the tree, he thinks this valuable piece of information will interest the group of boys he wants to join. At the same time Ricky begins to consider, with unsettling yet uncertain feelings, what the loss of the tree will mean to him. Philippa Pearce's story offers us a picture of a young boy who accompanies a group of friends on an innocent adventure that results in the loss of a cherished part of his world. Maybe moving out into a larger world means leaving certain things behind—but what is it that we give up along the way?

The Tree in the Meadow
by Philippa Pearce

THERE WERE BUILDINGS on three sides of Miss Mortlock's meadow; on the fourth, the river. In the middle of
the meadow stood the elm. There were other trees in the
meadow: sycamore, ash, horse chestnut. The elm was giant among them. It had always stood there. Nobody remembered its being younger than it was; nobody remembered it less than its present immense height. Nobody
really thought about it anymore. They saw it, simply.

Then one day a branch fell from the elm tree. It
seemed just to tear itself off from the main body of the
tree. There was nothing to show why, except for a discol-
oration of wood at the torn end.

At its thickest, the branch that fell was almost the
thickness of a man's body.

The fall caused some surprise in the houses overlooking the meadow; but nobody thought more about the in-
cident until—no, not the next year, but the year after that
—another branch dropped. The meadow had been cut for
hay, and the Scarr children had been making hay houses.
They had just gone in to tea when the branch—quite as
big as the previous one—fell. It fell where they had been
playing, smashing and scattering their hay houses. Mrs.
Scarr was very much upset at what might have happened
—at what *would* have happened if the children had still
been playing there. Mr. Scarr agreed that the possibilities
were upsetting; and he now pointed out that the rooks no
longer nested in the elm. *They* knew. Someday—one day
before too long—the whole tree would fall. It would fall

without warning, and the damage could only be guessed at. The elm might fall on Miss Mortlock's house; it might fall on the Scarrs' house; it might fall on the buildings the other side—old Mortlock stables and outhouses, no great loss if they were smashed, but a mess. Or—if everyone had great good luck—the elm might fall harmlessly away from all buildings, across the meadow toward the river.

Miss Mortlock was now told that she ought to have the elm taken down.

Miss Mortlock said that the elm had been there long before she was born and she hoped and expected that it would be there after she was dead. She wanted no advice on the subject.

Another branch fell from the elm tree, partly squashing a farm trailer. The farmer whose trailer it was had been renting the meadow from Miss Mortlock for his cows. He tried to make Miss Mortlock pay the value of the trailer. Miss Mortlock replied that he had left his trailer in a particularly foolish place. She could not be held responsible. Everyone knew what elm trees were like, especially when they were getting old and rotten. No doubt he had heard of previous branches falling.

Mr. Scarr had another conversation with Miss Mortlock about having the elm tree felled. She said that these tree surgeons, as they called themselves, used fancy equipment so that they could charge fancy prices. She could not afford them.

Mr. Scarr said that he knew two handymen, pals, with a crosscut saw, axe, wedges, and good rope. They could fell any tree to within six inches of where it should go. Miss Mortlock was surprised and delighted to hear that there was anybody who would come and do anything well, nowadays. Through Mr. Scarr, a bargain was struck between Miss Mortlock and the handymen.

Mr. Scarr told his family about the arrangement at supper. Mrs. Scarr sighed with relief and thought no more of it—until later. The little girls were too young to understand. Only Ricky was interested. He said: "What will happen to the tree?"

His father stared at him. "It'll be felled. Didn't you hear me?"

"I mean, what will happen to the tree after that?" He had once seen a truck passing through the village carrying an enormous tree trunk, lopped of all its branches, chained down.

"It won't be a tree when it's felled," said Mr. Scarr. "Timber. Poor timber, in this case. Not sound enough even for coffins. Not worth cartage."

That night Ricky looked out of his bedroom window over the meadow to the elm. It stood, a tree. It was leafless, at this time of year, and the outer twigs on one side made what you could think of as the shape of a woman's head with fluffed-out hair, face bent downward. He had seen that woman from his window ever since he could remember.

He tried to imagine the elm tree cut down; not there. He tried to imagine space where the trunk and branches and twigs were—the whole great shape missing from the meadow. He tried to imagine looking right across the meadow without the interruption of the tree; looking across emptiness to the stables on the other side. He could not.

The next day, on his way to school, Ricky called as usual for Willy Jim, his best friend, who lived at the top of the lane. They went on together, and Ricky said: "Our elm's being cut down."

"So what?" said Willy Jim, preoccupied. He was still Ricky's best friend, perhaps, but he was also in with a new gang at school. Ricky wanted to get into the same gang. He meant to try anyway.

In the playground later, Ricky said to Bones Jones, who was leader of the gang: "Our elm tree's going to be cut down. It's hundreds of years old; it's hundreds of feet high."

"Didn't know you owned an elm."

"Well, the elm in our meadow."

"Didn't know you owned a meadow."

"Oh, well—Miss Mortlock's meadow. She lets us play in it. Shall I let you know when they're going to cut the elm down?"

"If you like."

Later still that day, Toffy, a friend of Bones Jones, spoke to Ricky, which he did not often bother to do. He said: "I hope they cut that tree down after school, or on a Saturday. Otherwise we'll miss it." So Bones Jones had told Toffy and the others.

And when they were all going home from school, Bones Jones called to Ricky: "Don't forget to find out about what you said. Might be worth watching."

Surprisingly Ricky had difficulty in getting his piece of information. His father was vague, even mysterious, about when exactly the elm would be felled. He glanced several times at his wife, during Ricky's questioning. She listened in silence, grim.

So Ricky first knew when, looking out of his window just after getting up one morning, he saw a truck in the meadow, with a ladder on its roof, and two men unloading gear that would clearly turn out to be saw, axe, wedges, and rope.

At breakfast his mother said to his father: "If they start now, they'll have finished before the afternoon, won't they?"

"Likely," said Mr. Scarr.

"So that wicked tree'll be safely down by the time you get home from school," his mother said to Ricky. Ricky scowled.

But there was still one chance, and Ricky thought it worth taking.

On the way to school he told Willy Jim; in the playground he told Bones Jones, Toffy, and the two others who made up the gang. "They're starting on the elm this morning. If we go to the meadow between the end of school lunch and the beginning of afternoon school, we might be lucky. We might see the fall."

The older children were allowed out of school after lunch to go to the candy store. The six boys would need only to turn right toward the lane, instead of left toward the candy store, when they set off at the permitted time. They would have about twenty minutes.

So, between one o'clock and a quarter past, the whole gang, including Ricky, were tearing down the lane to Miss Mortlock's meadow. They halted at the meadow gate, surprised; Ricky himself felt abashed. The truck and handymen had gone, although wheel tracks showed they had been there. The elm still stood. At first sight, nothing had happened or was going to happen.

Then they noticed something about the base of the tree. They climbed the gate and went over. A wide gash had been chopped out of the trunk on the side toward the

river. On the opposite side, at the same level, the tree had
been sawed almost half through.

Ricky, remembering his father's talk, said: "They'll
drive the wedges in there, where they've sawed. When the
time comes."

It now occurred to them to wonder where *they* were—
the handymen, the tree fellers. Toffy recollected having
noticed a truck going up the village in the direction of
The Peacock. The handymen, having done most of the
hard work, had probably gone to get a beer at The Peacock. After that, they would come back and finish the
job.

Meanwhile, the boys had the elm tree to themselves.

They were examining the saw cut, all except for Ricky.
He had gone around almost to the other side of the tree.
Clasping the trunk with his arms, he pressed his body
close against it, tipped his head back, and let his gaze go
mountaineering up into the tree—up—up—

Then he saw it, and wondered that he had not noticed
it at once: the rope. It had been secured to the main part
of the tree as near to the top as possible. Its length fell
straight through the branches to the ground, passing near
the fingertips of one of his hands. It reached the ground,
where more of it—much more of it—lay at the foot of the
tree, coiled around and ready for use.

"Look!" said Ricky.

The others came around the tree and gathered where
the rope fell, staring at it; then staring up into the tree, to
where the end was fastened; then staring across the
meadow toward the river.

Bones Jones said: "We could take the rope out over the
meadow. That wouldn't do any harm."

Toffy said: "Not with us not pulling on it."

Willy Jim said: "And not with the wedges not in."

Ricky said nothing.

All the same they were very careful to take the loose end of the rope over the meadow toward the river, keeping as far as possible from the buildings on either side. They walked backward towards the river, dragging the rope. At first, it dragged slackly through the rough grass of the meadow. Then, as they walked with it, it began to lift a little from the ground. They still walked, and the deep, floppy curve of it began to grow shallower and shallower—nearer and nearer to a straight line running from the boys to the top of the elm tree. They pulled it almost taut, and paused.

Toffy said: "This is about where they'll stand."

Bones Jones said: "And pull."

They arranged themselves in what seemed to them a correct order along the rope, with the heaviest at the end. That was Bones Jones himself. Then came Toffy, then the other two and Willy Jim, and lastly Ricky, the lightest of all, nearest to the tree.

"And pull," repeated Bones Jones; and they pulled very gently, slightly tautening the rope, so that it ran from their hands in that straight, straight line to the top of the elm tree.

The cows that were grazing in the meadow had moved off slowly but intently to the farthest distance, against the old stables.

"Only the pulling would have to be in time," said Bones Jones. "You know: one, two, three, *pull,* rest; one, two, three, *pull,* rest. Feeling the sway of the tree, once it started swaying. Before it falls."

Miss Mortlock's dog, a King Charles spaniel, appeared at the gate into the meadow and stared at the boys. He was old and he didn't like boys, but this was his meadow. He came through the gate and toward what was going on. He stood between the tree and the boys, but some way off, watching. After a while he sat down, with the regretful slowness of someone who has forgotten to bring his shooting stick.

They were getting the rhythm now, slow but strong: "One, two, three, and *pull*, rest: one, two, three, and *pull*, rest. . . ." They were chanting in perfect time under their breaths; in perfect time they were pulling, gently, well.

Mrs. Scarr, looking up from her sink and out through the kitchen window, might have seen them; but the sweetbriar hedge was in the way.

Miss Mortlock did see them, from an upper window. She had gone up to take an after-lunch nap on her bed, and was about to draw the curtains. She looked out. Her eyesight was not good nowadays, but she knew boys when she saw them, and she knew at once what they must be doing. She saw that the elm tree was beginning a slow, graceful waving of its topmost branches. Very slightly: this-a-way; that-a-way. Only each time it swayed, the sway was more this-a-way, toward the river, than that-a-way, toward the house.

This-a-way; that-a-way . . .

Miss Mortlock knocked on the windowpane with her knuckles, but the boys could not hear the distant tapping. She called, but they could not hear her old woman's voice. She tried to push open the window, but that window had not been opened at the bottom for twenty years, and it was not going to be rushed now.

This-a-way; that-a-way; *this*-a-way—that-a-way—

"*Pull* . . . ," the boys chanted, ". . . and *pull* . . . and *pull.* . . ."

They did not hear the sound of the truck driving up to the meadow gate again. The two handymen saw. They began to shout even before they were out of the truck: "No!"

The cows lifted their heads to look toward the elm.

"Oh, no!" cried Miss Mortlock from the wrong side of the window glass.

The King Charles spaniel stood up and began to growl.

". . . and *pull* . . . and *pull* . . ."

"No!" whispered Ricky to himself.

For the rope they pulled on was no longer taut, even when they pulled it. It came slackly to them. There was a great, unimaginable creak, and then the elm began to lean courteously toward them. They stood staring; and the tree leaned over—over—reaching its tallness to reach them; and they saw what only the birds and the airplanes had ever seen before—the very crown of the tree, and it was roaring down toward them—

"NO!" screamed Ricky, who was nearest to it, seeing right into those reaching topmost branches that only the birds and the airplanes saw; and the other boys were yelling and scattering, and Miss Mortlock's window shot up suddenly and she was calling shrilly out of it, and the handymen were vaulting the gate and shouting, and the King Charles spaniel was barking, and the elm tree that had stood forever was crashing to the ground, and Ricky was running, running, running from it, and then tripped and fell face forward into the nettles on the riverbank and staggered to his feet to run again, but suddenly there was nothing to run on, and fell again. Into the river this time.

The river was not deep or swift-flowing, but muddy.

He wallowed and floundered to the bank and clawed a hold there and stood, thigh-deep in water, against the bank, still below visibility from the meadow. He listened. There were the mingled sounds of boys shouting and men shouting and a dog barking. He guessed that the men were chasing the boys, and the dog was getting in the way.

But he didn't stay. He waded along the river, in the shelter of the vegetation on its bank, until he reached the end of the meadow. The boundary of the meadow, on this side, was a sweetbriar hedge that, farther up, became the hedge of the Scarrs' garden. He crept out, and crept home.

His face tingled all over and had already swollen— even to the eyelids—with nettle stings, and he was dripping with river water and with river mud that stank. His mother, meeting him at the door, and having—at last; who could miss it now?—realized what had happened in the meadow, dealt with him.

No question of his going back to afternoon school: he ended up in bed. His mother rattled the curtains together angrily and told him to stay exactly where he was until his dad came home.

When she had gone, he slid out of bed and laid a hand on the curtains to part them. But he did not. There was no sound of voices from the meadow now; and he didn't really want to see. He had thought he wanted to, but he did not. He went back to bed.

His father, home for tea, was far less angry than his mother. He liked the idea of half a dozen schoolboys felling the elm tree by accident—and Ricky among them. "Didn't think you had it in you," he said to Ricky.

As for punishment, the state of Ricky's face was about as much as was needed, in Mr. Scarr's opinion.

And anyway, said Mr. Scarr, nobody had expressly told the boy not to fell the tree. Then Mrs. Scarr became very angry with Mr. Scarr, as well as with Ricky.

Next day at school there was a row, but not too bad. It was over quickly. The rest of the gang had had theirs yesterday. In the playground Willy Jim said to Ricky, "You can go around with us, Bones says. We call ourselves Hell Fellows now—Hell Fellers—*fellers:* get it?"

"Oh," said Ricky, "you're one?"

"Yes," said Willy Jim, "and you can be one, too."

So that was all right, of course. Ricky had what he wanted.

Bones Jones decided that after school the Hell Fellers would go and look at the tree they had felled. No use going straight from school, however, as Ricky said, because the men would be there, lopping and sawing. So they all went home first to their teas, and then reassembled, singly, carefully casual, at the top of the lane—all except for Ricky, of course, who had had his tea and then hung over his front gate, waiting.

When daylight began to fail, the handymen stopped work, packed everything into the truck, shut the meadow gate, and drove away. They drove out of the top of the lane, and behind them, the boys converged on the entrance to the lane and poured down it. They collected Ricky as they passed his house, then over the meadow gate and across the meadow to the elm.

Most of its branches had already gone, so that they could clamber up it and along it fairly easily. Bones Jones, Willy Jim, Ricky—all of them—they clambered, climbed on and jumped off, ran along the trunk. They fought duels along the trunk with lopped-off branches and nearly put each other's eyes out; played a no-holds-barred King of the Castle on the tree stump; carved their initials in the thickness of the main bark. All they did, they did quietly—with whispers, gasps, grunts, suppressed laughter—for they did not wish to call attention to themselves. There was little fear, otherwise, of their being noticed in the half-light.

Now they gathered together in a line along the trunk. Ricky was in the middle. They linked arms and danced, stamping and singing softly together a song of victory, of Hell Fellers, hell-bent, of victors over the vanquished. The stamping of their feet hardly shook the massive tree trunk beneath them.

The meadow was almost dark now. Like ghosts they danced along the long ghost of what had once been a tree.

Oblongs of yellow light had appeared in the houses overlooking the meadow. The dancers began to waver. They shivered at the chill of night, and remembered their homes. They stopped dancing. They left the tree trunk, climbed the gate, went home.

Ricky went home. He was still humming the tune to which they had danced. "You seem pleased with yourself," his mother said grumpily. She had not got over yesterday. Ricky said, "Yes."

When he was going to bed, he looked out of his window, across the meadow. It was quite dark outside, but you could still see which was sky and which was not. He could make out the blackness of the old stables against the sky. There was nothing between him and them. He stared till his eyes watered.

He got into bed thinking of tomorrow and the Hell Fellers at school, pleased. He fell asleep at once, and began dreaming. His own tears woke him. He could not remember his dream, and knew that it had not lasted long, because the same television program was still going on downstairs.

In the middle of being puzzled at grief he fell asleep again.

Walter D. Edmonds, "Water Never Hurt a Man"

For young John Brace, becoming a driver boy on the Erie Canal offers a new pair of boots, his first dollar in wages paid in advance, and the pride of working with his father, who is both feared and respected along the canal. But that first spring guiding the horses through the squudging mud of the towpath attacks his enthusiasm with exhaustion, anger, and fear. Here, on a night darkened by storm and lit only dimly by a boat lantern or briefly by bursts of lightning, John does his best just to protect himself and winds up gaining his father's respect.

Opened in 1825, the 363-mile Erie Canal provided a link for travelers and goods across New York State between Albany on the east (and down the Hudson River to New York City) and Buffalo on the west (then, by way of Lake Erie, to the interior of the growing country). Edmonds's dramatically lit story takes us at the towing team's pace along a section of that canal with a twelve-year-old boy struggling to succeed in his new role.

Water Never Hurt a Man
by Walter D. Edmonds

HE TRUDGED WITH his hands tight fists in his pockets, his head bowed to the wind and rain. Ahead of him in the darkness, so that he could hear the squudge of their hoofs, the towing team bowed their necks against the collars. He could not see them in the darkness. When he lifted his face, the rain cut at his eyes; and when lightning split the darkness he shut his eyes tight and pulled his head closer into his coat collar, waiting blindly for the thunder. Once in a lull he looked back. He could barely make out the bow lantern and the arrows of gray rain slanting against it. Between him and the light he caught glimpses of the towrope, dipped slightly between the team's heaves, and the roughened water in the canal. Somewhere behind the light his father stood by the rudder sweep, his beard curled and wet, his eyes slits, sighting for the bank. John wanted to go back, wanted to tie-by for the night, wanted to be in the bunk with his head buried in the friendly, musty smell of the blanket, where the storm could not reach him. He had gone back once, but his father had reached for his belt, saying, "Go on back. Watter never hurt a man. It keeps his hide from cracking."

John had gone back to the team. They did not need his guidance. But it was his place to keep the rope from fouling if a packet boat coming their way signaled to pass. He was afraid of his father at night, afraid of the big belt and strong hands with hair on the fingers over the knuckles. He caught up with the plodding horses and let the rain have its way. At each stroke of lightning his small back stiffened. It was his first year on the canal and he was afraid of storms at night.

He had been proud that spring when his father said, "John's old enough to be a driver boy; he's coming along with me and the *Bacconola.*" He had showed his dollar to his brothers and sisters, first pay in advance, and his father had bought him a pair of cowhide boots from the cobbler when he came to the village. Later, when the frost was out of the mud, John would go barefoot.

He was proud of his father. In Westernville, with other small boys, he had heard the dock loafers talking about his father, George Brace, bully of the Black River Canal. In some strange way they had news of every fight his father fought a day after it happened. "George licked the Amsterdam Bully Wednesday mornin'. Lock fifty-nine. It tuk nineteen minits only." "George is a great hand. Them big ditch bezabors is learning about George." A stranger had said, "Wait till Buffalo Joe meets up with him." There was silence then. Buffalo Joe Buller, he was bully of the western end of the Erie. A pea souper, a Canadian, he fought the Erie bullies down one by one, and when he licked them he marked them with his boot in the Canadian style. It had a cross of nails to mark the beaten man's face. "You wait," said the stranger.

Little John, listening, felt shivers down his back. But now, with the wind and rain, and the lightning tumbling the clouds apart, he forgot. They were on the long haul westward, to Buffalo, with ploughs aboard, full-drafted in Rome. They had had to leave three-hundredweight on the dock.

He felt his muddy boots slip in the towpath. He heard the squelching of the horses. Squelch-squelch, a steady rhythm as they kept step. Once the lightning caught his eyes; and he had a clear view of trees beyond the canal-side meadow, their budded twigs bent down like old women with their backs to the storm, and the flat, sharp wall of a canal house sixty yards behind him. He had not even seen it as he passed. The rain was finding a channel down his neck. It crept farther, bit by bit, with a cold touch. He could feel his fists white in his pockets from clenching them. His legs ached with the slippery going. They had had supper at six, tied up by the bank, and John had eaten his plate of beans. He had felt sleepy afterward, barely noticing his father's big body bent over the dishpan. It was warm in the cabin, with the little stove roaring red hot, and his small hat hanging beside his father's cap on the door.

He had been almost asleep when his father's hand shook him roughly, then tumbled him from his chair. "Get out, John. Them ploughs we've got has to get west for spring ploughing. We'll pick up Bob in Syracuse, then we'll have a better chance to rest. Get out now," and he had reached for his belt.

What did John care for the old ploughs anyway? But it hadn't then begun to storm, and he had gone, with a tired sense of importance. One had to keep freight moving on the old Erie. The old *Bacconola* always made fast hauls. He had been proud and shouted in a high voice to the tired horses and kicked one with his new boots.

But now he did not care about the ploughs. He wished the crazy old *Bacconola* would spring a leak in her flat bottom, so they would have to stop till the hurry-up boat came along and patched her up. He thought of her now, bitterly, with her scabs of orange paint. "Crummy old blister," he called her to himself and made names for her, which he said aloud to the horses in a shrill voice. He was only twelve, with all the bitterness of twelve, and the world was a hateful thing.

"God-damned old crummy bitch of a tub . . ." But the lightning caught him, and his throat tightened and he wanted to cry out under the thunder.

A water rat went off the towpath with a splash, and a frog squeaked.

He glanced up to see a team on the opposite towpath heading east. "Hey, there!" yelled the driver in a hoarse voice; but John was too tired to answer. He liked to yell back in the daytime and crack his whip. But he had dropped his whip a while back. He would get a licking for that in the morning. But he didn't care. To hell with the whip and the driver and Pa!

"Hey, there!" shouted the other driver, a voice in the rain. "All right, all right, you dirty pup. Eat rain, if you want to, and go drownd." The rain took the voice, and the boat came by, silently, noiseless as oil, with its bow light a yellow touch against the rain. The steersman gave a toot upon the horn, but the sound bubbled through the water in it, and the steersman swore.

They were still on the long level, alone once more. It must be midnight. If only the lock would show. In Syracuse, Bob would come. He took turns driving and steering and cooking—a little man with a bent shoulder who had dizzy spells once in a while.

At the lock John could sit down and rest and listen to the tender snarling at his sluices while the boat went down, and heaving at his gate beam, while John's father heaved against the other. He was crazy, the lockkeeper was; all lockkeepers were crazy. John's father always said so. John had seen a lot of them in their week of hauling, but he did not see why they were crazy. They looked no different even if they were. He hoped the lockkeeper would be asleep, so it would take a while to wake him.

Squelch, squelch-squelch, squelch. The horses kept plodding. Suddenly John caught a break in the rhythm. One foot sounded light. He pushed his way up beside them against the wind and laid a wet hand against a side. He could not see, but the side felt hot and wet, and he got a smell of sweat. Yes, he could feel the off horse limping. Hope filled him. He waited till the boat came up where he was, a small figure, shrunk with cold. The boat's bow, round and sullen, slipped along, the bow light hanging over and showing an old mullein stalk in silhouette against the water.

"Pa!"

His voice was thin against the wind.

He saw his father's figure, rain dripping from the visor of his cap, straight and big, almighty almost, breast to the wind.

"Pa!"

The head turned.

"Hey, there! What you doin'? Get on back, or I'll soap you proper!"

"Pa! Prince has got a limp in his front foot. Pa!"

The voice turned hoarse with passion. "Get on back, you little pup! Fifty-nine's just round the next bend. Take your whip and tar him, or I'll tar you proper."

John sobbed aloud. For a bare moment he thought of staying still and letting the boat pass on. He would run away and join the railroad. He would get run over by an engine there, just when things went well, and they would be sorry. He started to draw himself a picture of his body coming home in a black box, and his mother crying, and his father looking ashamed and sorry, and then the lightning made a blue flare and he saw the straight figure of his father ahead, on the *Bacconola,* which seemed struck still, a pillbox in the flat country, and he was afraid and went running desperately, hoping he could get back to the team before he was missed.

He caught the horses on the bend and, lifting his face to the storm, saw the lock lanterns dimly ahead. And even then his ears caught, coming up behind him, the harsh blast of a tin horn.

He looked back and saw a light, two rope lengths behind the *Bacconola.* Even while he watched over his shoulder, he saw that it was creeping up.

"John!" His father's voice beat down the sound of rain. "Lay into them brutes and beat into the lock!"

He could imagine his father glaring back. If only he had not dropped his whip. He would have liked to ask his father for the big bull whip that cracked like forty guns, but he knew what would happen if he did. He shrieked at the horses and fumbled for a stone to throw. But they had heard and recognized the note in his father's voice, and they were bending earnestly against the collars. A sudden excitement filled John as his father's horn rang out for the lock. The wind took the sound and carried it back, and the other boat's horn sounded a double toot for passing. John yelled shrilly. The horses seemed to stand still, and there was an odd effect in the rain of the canal sliding under them inch by inch laboriously, as if with his own feet he turned the world backward.

Minutes crept at them out of the rain, and the lights of the lock did not seem to stir. Then John heard the squelching of the team behind his back. Little by little they were coming up, past the *Bacconola,* until he could hear them panting through the rain, and saw them close behind, behind dim puffs of steamy breath. He watched them frantically. Then the lightning came once more, a triple bolt, and the thunder shook him, and when he opened his eyes once more he saw the lock lanterns a hundred yards ahead.

At that instant the driver of the boat behind yelled, "Haw!" and the following team swung across his towrope and they were snarled.

The horses stopped of themselves, shuddering. They were old hands, and knew enough not to move, for fear of being thrown from the towpath. The boats came drifting on, placidly as waterlogged sticks. The light of the following boat showed a dark bow coming up. John heard his father roaring oaths, and saw by the bow light of the other boat a tall, clean-shaven man as big as his father, crouched to jump ashore. Then both boats came in by the towpath, and both men jumped. They made no sound except for the thump of their shoes, but John saw them dim against the lantern light, their fists coming at each other in slow, heavy swings.

The strange team was panting close beside him, and he did not hear the blows landing. There was a pushing upward in his chest, which hurt, and his fists made small balls in the pockets of his trousers. The other boater and his father were standing breast to breast, their faces still, cut, stonelike things in the yellow light, and the rain walling them in. He saw his father lift his hand, and the other man slip, and he would have yelled, for all his cold, if the lightning had not come again, so blue that his eyes smarted. He doubled up, hiding his face, and wept. . . .

A hand caught him by the shoulder.

"A little puny girly boy," said a voice. "I wouldn't lick

you proper! Not a little girly baby like you. But I'll spank you just to learn you to let us come by!"

John opened his eyes to see a boy, about his own height, but broader built, squinting at him through the rain.

"Take off your pants, dearie," said the boy in a mock voice, digging in his fingers till John winced. "Joe Buller can handle your captain smart enough. Me, I'll just paddle you to learn you."

John, looking up, was afraid. He did not know what to do, but without warning his hands acted for him, and he struck at the square face with all his might. A pain shot up his arm, making his elbow tingle, and the boy fell back. John could feel the surprise in that body stock-still in the rain, and had an instant of astonished pride.

Then panic laid hold of him and he tried to run. But the other boy jumped on his back. They went down flat in the mud, the older boy on John's shoulders, pummeling him till his head sang, and forcing his face into the track, and crying, "Eat it, you lousy little skunk! Eat it, eat it, eat it, eat it!"

John could taste the mud in his mouth, with a salty taste, and he began to squirm, twisting his head to escape the brown suffocation. He heaved himself behind, throwing the boy unexpectedly forward, twisted round, and kicked with all his might. The boy yelled and jumped back on him. And again they went down; this time the boy bent seriously to business. And this time John realized how it was to be hurt. At the third blow something burst loose in his inside and he screamed. He was crying madly. The other boy was heavier, but John squirmed over on his back, and as the brown hand came down on his face he caught it in both his own and bit with all the strength of his jaws. The hand had a slippery, muddy taste, but in a second it was warm in his mouth, and there was a sick, salt wetness on his tongue. The boy struck him once in the eyes and once on the nose, but John held on and bit. Then the boy howled and tore loose and ran back. There was another stroke of lightning, and John saw him doubled up, holding his hand to his mouth; and he got stiffly up, turned his back to the thunder, and saw his father bent over the other boater, taking off his shoe.

John walked up to them. His father's face was bleeding a trickle of blood from the right eye into his beard, but he was grinning.

"I'll take his boot for a souvenir," he said. "How'd you come out, Johnny?"

"Oh, pretty good. I guess that other feller won't bother us no more," said John, examining the fallen man. He lay half stunned, by the water's edge, a smooth, big man, with frightened, pale eyes. And one crumpled arm was in the water. John's father looked at the man and then at the boot he had in his hand.

"I'd ought to mark him by the rights of it; but he ain't worth the work, the way he láid down. Who'd ever know his name was Buller?"

Buller. . . . John gazed up admiringly at his big father and studied how the blood ran from the outer corner of the eye and lost its way in the black beard, which the rain had curled. His father had licked the western bully proper.

"Hey, there!"

The hail came in a thin, cracking voice. Turning, they saw the lockkeeper, white bearded, peering at them from under the battered umbrella he held with both hands against the wind. The tails of his nightshirt whipped round the tops of his boots.

"Hey, there, you. There'll be some down boats by pretty quick, so you want to hurry along now, while the level's right."

John was aware of his father standing looking down at him.

"Shall we tie-by where we be?" asked his father.

John felt pains coming into the back of his neck where he had been pummeled, and his knuckles ached.

"We can stay here a spell," said his father. "The storm's comin' on again. There'll be bad lightnin', I make no doubt."

As he spoke there came a flash, and John whirled to see if the other driver boy was still visible. He was proud to see him sitting by the towpath, nursing his hurt hand. John did not notice the thunder. He was elaborating a sentence in his mind.

He made a hole in the mud with the toe of his boot, spat into it, and covered it, the way he had seen his father do at home on a Sunday.

"Why," he said, in his high voice, eying the old *Bacconola,* "I guess them poor bezabor farmers will be wantin' them ploughs for the spring ploughing, I guess."

"Me, I'm kind of tuckered," said his father, raising his shoulders to loose the wet shirt off his back. "And the rain's commencing, too."

John said importantly, "Watter never hurt a man; it keeps his hide from cracking."

His father jumped aboard. He took his horn and tooted it for the lock. John ran ahead and put back the other boat's team and cried to their own horses to go on. They took up the slack wearily, and presently little ripples showed on the *Bacconola*'s bow, and the lantern showed the shore slipping back. On the stern George Brace blew a blast for the lock. The old lockkeeper was standing by the sluices, drops of water from his beard falling between his feet.

The boat went down, and the horses took it out. Ahead, the team and the boy left the lantern light and entered once more the darkness. The rope followed. And once more the *Bacconola* was alone with its own lantern.

Presently, though, in a stroke of light, George saw his son beside the boat.

"What's the matter? Hey, there!" he asked.

"Say, Pa! Will you chuck me your bull whip here ashore? Them horses is getting kind of dozy. They need soaping proper."

"Where's your whip?"

"I guess I left it awhile back. I guess it was in that kind of scrummage we had. I guess it needs a heavier whip anyhow. I guess a man couldn't spare the time going back for it."

"Sure," said George.

He reached down and took it from its peg, recoiled it, and tossed it ashore. The boat went ahead, slowly, with a sound of water, and of rain falling, and of wind.

E. L. Konigsburg, "On Shark's Tooth Beach"

Ned Hixon figures that he and his mother don't need any advertisement as the local authorities on the fossils that wash up on the beach near their Florida home. People find out sooner or later. But somehow Bob ("Did I tell you that I was president of a college?") Kennicott misses the message. Not only does President Bob fail to recognize Ned's authority as Ned sees fit, but he also begins with some success to challenge Ned's supremacy on the beach. E. L. Konigsburg has chosen Ned to tell his own story, tracing the changes he experiences in this two-week battle. And if the picture Ned paints of President Bob—a self-important, presumptuous old man on spindly vanilla legs—is not a flattering one, consider the view Ned offers of himself as he comes to understand his part in the mounting struggle and finally achieves a victory of an unexpected sort.

On Shark's Tooth Beach
by E. L. Konigsburg

MY DAD IS Hixon of Hixon's Landing, the fishing camp down on the intracoastal waterway just across Highway A1A. Our camp isn't a fancy one. Just two coolers, one for beer and one for bait, plus four boats, and eight motors that we rent out.

Dad was raised on a farm in Nebraska, but he joined the Navy and signed on for the war in Vietnam and came back knowing two things. One, he hated war, and two, he loved the sea. Actually, he came back with two loves. The other one was my mother. There wasn't *any* way *any*one could get him to settle *any*where that was far from the ocean when he got out of the service, so he bought this small stretch of land in north Florida, and we've been there for all of my life that I can remember.

Dad's got this small pension for getting wounded over in Nam, so between what we sell, what we rent, and what the government sends, we do all right. We're not what you're likely to call rich, but we are all right. Mom doubts that we'll ever make enough money to pay for a trip to her native country of Thailand, but she doesn't seem to mind. She says that it is more important to love where you're at than to love where you're from.

Mom makes and sells sandwiches for the fishermen. She does a right good job on them, I can tell you. There is this about Mom's sandwiches: you don't have to eat half-way through to the middle to find out what's between the bread, and once you get hold of a bite, you don't have to guess at whether it is egg salad or tuna that you're eating. The filling is high in size and in flavor.

The town next door to us is spreading south toward our landing, and both Mom and Dad say that our property will be worth a pretty penny in a few years. But both of them always ask, "What's a pretty penny worth when you can't buy anything prettier than what you already have?" I have to agree. Maybe because I don't know anything else, but I can't imagine what it would be like not to have a sandbox miles and miles long and a pool as big as an ocean for a playground across the street—even if the street is a highway. I can't ever remember going to sleep but that I heard some water shushing and slurping or humming and hollering for a lullaby.

Last spring, just as the days were getting long enough that a person could both start and finish something between the time he got home from school and the time he went to bed, I went out onto our dock and I saw this guy all duded up from a catalogue. Now that the town has grown toward us, we have more of these guys than we used to. When you've been in the business of fishing all your life, you come to know the difference between fishermen and guys who have a hobby. Here are some of the clues:

1. The hat. A real fisherman's hat is darkened along the edges where the sweat from his hand leaves marks. A nonfisherman's hat has perfect little dent marks in it.

2. The smile. Real fishermen don't smile while they're fishing unless someone tells them a joke. Real fishermen wear their faces in the same look people wear when they are in church—deliberate and far-off—the way they do when they don't want to catch the eye of the preacher. The only time that look changes is when they take a swig

of beer and then it changes only a little and with a slow rhythm like watching instant replay on television. Nonfishermen twitch their necks around like pigeons, which are very citified birds, and nonfishermen smile a lot.

3. The umbrella. Real fishermen don't have them.

This old guy sat on a wooden-legged, canvas-bottom folding campstool that didn't have any salt burns on it anywhere and put his rod into one of the holders that Dad had set up along the dock railing. Then he held out his hand and called out, "Hey, boy, do you know what I've got here?"

I walked on over to him and said, "Name's Ned."

"What's that?" he asked, cupping his hand over his ear so that the breeze wouldn't blow it past him.

"I said that my name is Ned," I repeated.

"All right, Ed," he said. "I have a question for you. Do you know what this is, boy?"

"Name's Ned," I repeated. I looked down at the palm of his hand and saw a medium-sized shark's tooth from a sand shark. "Not bad," I said.

"But do you know what it is, boy?" he asked.

I could tell that it wasn't the kind of question where a person is looking for an answer; it was the kind of question where a person just wants you to look interested long enough so that he can get on with telling you the answer. I decided that I wouldn't play it that way even if he was a customer. Three *boys* in a row made me mean, so I said, "Medium-sized sand."

"What's that?" he shouted, cupping his hand over his ear again.

"Medium-sized sand," I repeated louder.

"That's a shark's tooth," he said, clamping his hand shut.

Shoot! I knew that it was a shark's tooth. I was telling him what *kind* it was and what size it was.

"That is a fossilized shark's tooth, boy," he said. "Found it just across the street."

"Name's Ned," I told him, and I walked away.

Sharks' teeth wash up all the time at the beach just across the road from Hixon's Landing. There's a giant fossil bed out in the ocean somewheres, and a vent from it leads right onto our beach. When the undertow gets to digging up out of that fossil bed and the tide is coming in, all kinds of interesting things wash in. Besides the sharks' teeth, there are also pieces of bones that wash up. I collect the backbones, the vertebraes, they're called; they have a hole in them where the spinal column went through. I have a whole string of them fixed according to size.

I collect sharks' teeth too. I have been doing it for years. Mom started me doing it. It was Mom who made a study of them and found what kind of animal they might come from. Mom has these thorough ways about her. Dad says that Mom is smarter'n a briar and prettier'n a movie star.

Mom fixes the sharks' teeth that we collect into patterns and fastens them down onto a velvet mat and gets them framed into a shadowbox frame. She sells them down at the gift shop in town. And the gift shop isn't any tacky old gift shop full of smelly candles and ashtrays with the name of our town stamped on it. It's more like an art gallery. Matter of fact, it is called the Artists' Gallery, and Mom is something of an artist at how she makes those sharks' teeth designs. Some of the really pretty sharks' teeth Mom sells to a jeweler, who sets them in gold for pendants. When she gets two pretty ones that match, he makes them into earrings.

When I find her a really special or unusual one, Mom says to me, "Looks like we got a trophy, Ned." When we get us a trophy, one that needs investigating or one that is just downright super special, we don't sell it. Shoot! We don't even think about selling it. There's nothing that bit of money could buy that we'd want more than having that there trophy.

Most everyone who comes to Hixon's Landing knows about Mom and me being something of authorities on fossils, especially sharks' teeth, so I figured that this old dude would either go away and not come back or hang around long enough to find out. Either way, I figured that I didn't need to advertise for myself and my mom.

The next day after school there was the old fellow again. I wouldn't want to sound braggy or anything, but I could tell that he was standing there at the end of our dock waiting for me to come home from school.

"Hi," I said.

"Well, boy," he said, "did you have a good day at school?"

"Fair," I answered. I decided to let the *boy* ride. I figured that he couldn't hear or couldn't remember or both. "Catch anything?" I asked.

"No, not today," he said. "Matter of fact I was just about to close up shop." Then he began reeling in, looking back over his shoulder to see if I was still hanging around. He didn't even bother taking the hook off his line; he just dumped rod and reel down on the dock and stuck out his hand to me and said, "Well, son, you can call me President Bob."

"What are you president of?" I asked.

"President of a college, upstate Michigan. But I'm retired now."

"Then you're not a president," I said.

"Not at the moment, but the title stays. The way that people still call a retired governor, *Governor*. You can call me President Bob instead of President Kennicott. Bob is more informal, but I wouldn't want you to call me just Bob. It doesn't seem respectful for a boy to call a senior citizen just Bob."

"And you can call me Ned," I said. "That's my name."

"All right, son," he said.

"After the first day, I don't answer to *son* or to *boy*," I said.

"What did you say your name was, son?"

Shoot! He had to learn. So I didn't answer.

"What is your name again?"

"Ned."

"Well, Ned, would you like to take a walk on the beach and hunt for some of those sharks' teeth?"

"Sure," I said.

He must have counted on my saying yes, because the next thing I see is him dropping his pants and showing me a pair of skinny white legs with milky blue veins sticking out from under a pair of bathing trunks.

As we walked the length of the dock, he told me that he was used to the company of young men, since he had been president of a college. "Of course, the students were somewhat older," he said. Then he laughed a little, like punctuation. I didn't say anything. "And, of course, I didn't often see the students on a one-to-one basis." I didn't say anything. "I was president," he added. He glanced over at me, and I still didn't say anything. "I was president," he added.

"There's supposed to be some good fishing in Michigan," I said.

"Oh, yes! Yes, there is. Good fishing. Fine fishing. Sportsmen's fishing."

We crossed A1A and got down onto the beach from a path people had worn between the dunes, and I showed him how to look for sharks' teeth in the coquina. "There's nothing too much to learn," I said. "It's mostly training your eye."

He did what most beginners do, that is, he picked up a lot of wedge-shaped pieces of broken shell, mostly black, thinking they were fossil teeth. The tide was just starting on its way out, and that is the best time for finding sharks' teeth. He found about eight of them, and two of them were right nice sized. I found fourteen myself and three of mine were bigger than anything he collected. We compared, and I could tell that he was wishing he had mine, so I gave him one of my big ones. It wasn't a trophy or anything like that because I would never do that to Mom, that is, give away a trophy or a jewelry one.

President Bob was waiting for me the next day and the day after that one. By the time Friday afternoon came, President Bob gave up on trying to pretend that he was fishing. He'd just be there on the dock, waiting for me to take him sharks' tooth hunting.

"There's no magic to it," I told him. "You can go without me."

"That's all right, Ned," he said, "I don't mind waiting."

On Saturday I had a notion to sleep late and was in the process of doing just that when Mom shook me out of my sleep and told me that I had a visitor. It was President Bob, and there he was standing on his vanilla legs right by my bedroom door. He had gotten tired of waiting for me on the dock. It being Saturday, he had come early so's we could have more time together.

Mom invited him in to have breakfast with me, and while we ate, she brought out our trophy boxes. Our trophies were all sitting on cotton in special boxes like the ones you see butterflies fixed in inside a science museum. Mom explained about our very special fossils.

"Oh, yes," President Bob said. Then, "Oh, yes," again. Then after he'd seen all our trophies and had drunk a second cup of coffee, he said, "We had quite a fine reference library in my college. I am referring to the college of which I was president. Not my alma mater, the college I attended as a young man. We had quite a fine library, and I must confess I used it often, so I am not entirely unfamiliar with these things."

That's when I said, "Oh, yes," except that it came out "Oh, yeah!" and that's when Mom swiped my foot under the table.

President Bob plunked his empty cup down on the table and said, "Well, come on, now, Ned, time and tide wait for no man. Ha! Ha!"

I think that I've heard someone say that at least four times a week. Everyone says it. Dad told me that it was a proverb, an old, old saying. And I can tell you that it got old even before I reached my second birthday.

When we got down to the beach, President Bob brought out a plastic bag and flung it open like a bag boy at the supermarket. But there wasn't much to fill it with that day because the currents had shifted and weren't churning up the fossil bed.

CHAPTER II

"I suppose you'll be going to church tomorrow," he said.

"Yes," I answered.

"I think I'll do some fishing in the morning. I'll probably have had enough of that by noon. I'll meet you at the dock about twelve-thirty. We can get started on our shark's tooth hunt then."

"Sorry," I said. "I help Mom with the sandwiches and then we clean things up and then we go to late services. Sunday is our busiest day."

"Of course it is," he said.

Mom and I got back about one-thirty and changed out of our good clothes before Dad came in as he always does on Sundays to grab some lunch before the men start coming back and he has to get busy with washing down motors and buying. (What he buys is fish from the men who have had a specially good run. Dad cleans them and sells them to markets back in town or to people who drive on out toward the beach of a Sunday. Sometimes, he gets so busy buying and cleaning that Mom and I pitch right in and give him a hand.)

Dad had not quite finished his sandwiches and had just lifted his beer when he got called out to the dock. There was this big haul of bass that some men were wanting to sell.

Mom and I were anxious to finish our lunch and clean up so's we could go on out and see if Dad would be needing some help when President Bob presented himself at the screen door to our kitchen.

"Knock, knock," he said, pressing his old face up against the screen. The minute we both looked up he opened the door without even an *if you please* and marched into our kitchen on his frosted icicle legs. "I

think you're going to be interested in what I found today," he said. "Very interested."

Mom smiled her customer smile and said, "We are
having very busy day, please to excuse if I continue with
work."

"That's perfectly all right," President Bob said.
"You're excused." Then he sat down at the table that
Mom was wiping off. He held up the place mat and said,
"Over here, Mama-san. You missed a spot."

Mom smiled her customer smile again and wiped the
spot that he had pointed to, and President Bob put the
place mat back down and emptied the contents of his
plastic bag right on top of it. He leaned over the pile and,
using his forefinger, began to comb through it. "Ah!
here," he said. He picked up a small black thing between
his thumb and forefinger and said to Mom, "Come here,
Mama-san." *Mama-san* is some kind of Japanese for
mama. A lot of people call my mom that, but she says it's
okay because it is a term of respect, and a lot of people
think that all Orientals are Japanese. Sometimes these
same people call me Boy-san, which is to *boy* what
Mama-san is to mama. They call me that because I have
dark slanted eyes just like Mom's, except that hers are
prettier.

"Look at this," President Bob said. "Look at it closely.
I suspect that it is the upper palate of an extinct species of
deep-water fish."

Mom took it from his hand and looked at it and said,
"Dolphin tooth." She put it back down and walked to the
sink, where she continued right on with washing up the
dishes. She automatically handed me a towel to dry.

President Bob studied the dolphin's tooth and said to
Mom, "Are you sure?"

She smiled and nodded.

"Quite sure?"

She nodded.

He asked once more, and she nodded again. Then he began poking through his collection again and came up with another piece. He beckoned to Mom to look at it closer, and she dried her hands and did that.

"Shell," she said.

"Oh, I beg to differ with you," he said.

"Shell," Mom said, looking down at it, not bothering to pick it up.

"Are you sure?"

She nodded.

"Quite sure?"

She nodded again, and I came over and picked it up off the table and held it up and broke it in two. I thought that President Bob was going to arrest me. "A piece of fossil that thick wouldn't break that easy. It's a sure test," I said.

"There are fragile fossils, I'm sure," President Bob said.

"I suppose so," I said. "But that shell ain't fossilized. Piece of fossil that thick wouldn't ever break that easy." I could see that you had to repeat yourself with President Bob. "That shell ain't fossilized."

"*Ain't* is considered very bad manners up North," President Bob said.

Shoot! *Bad manners* are considered bad manners down South, I thought. But I didn't say anything. President Bob kept sorting through his bag of stuff, studying on it so hard that his eyes winched up and made his bottom jaw drop open.

Mom finished washing the dishes, and I finished dry-ing, and we asked if we could be excused, and President Bob told us (in our own kitchen, mind) that it was perfectly all right, but would we please fetch him a glass of ice water before we left. We fetched it. He said, "Thank you. You may go now." I suppose that up North it's good manners to give people orders in their own house if you do it with *please* and *thank you* and no *ain'ts*.

It rained on Monday and it rained again on Tuesday, so I didn't see President Bob again until Wednesday after school. He was waiting for me at the end of the dock with his plastic sandwich bag already partly full. "Well," he said, "I guess I got a bit of a head start on you today."

I looked close at his bag and saw that he had a couple of nice ones—not trophies—but nice.

"I have homework," I said. "I can't walk the beaches with you today."

"What subject?"

"Math."

"Maybe I can help you. Did I tell you that I was president of a college?"

"Really?" I said in my fakiest voice. "I think I better do my homework by myself."

"I'll wait for you," he said. "I promise I won't hunt for anything until you come back out."

"It'll probably take me the rest of daylight to do it," I said.

"Math must be hard for you," he said. "Always was my strongest subject."

"It's not hard for me," I lied. "I just have a lot of it."

"Let me show you what I found today," he said.

"I don't think I have the time."

"Just take a minute."

Before I could give him another polite no, he had

spread the contents of his bag over the railing of the dock. I looked things over real good. I knew he was watching me, so I wouldn't let my eyes pause too long on any one thing in particular. "Very nice," I said. "I've got to go now."

As I turned to walk back to our house, he called, "See you tomorrow."

The next day I didn't even walk to the dock. Instead I walked around to the side door of our house and threw my books on the wicker sofa on the screened porch and went up to my room and changed into my cutoffs. I had a plan; I was going to go back out the side door and walk a bit to the north before crossing the highway and climbing over the dunes onto the beach. I knew a place where a sandbar often formed, and Mom and I sometimes went there. When I was little, she'd put me in the sloop behind the sandbar, like at a wading pool at a regular Holiday Inn. As I got older, we'd go there on lazy days and take a picnic lunch and sift through the coquina of the sandbar. We've found about four trophies there. Not about, exactly four. Of the four, the first one was the most fun because it was the one we found by accident.

I felt if I could get out of the house and head north, I could escape President Bob and dig up some trophies that would make him flip.

But I didn't escape. When I came downstairs after changing my clothes, there he was sitting on the wicker sofa, his blueberry ripple legs crossed in front of him. He was leafing through my math book.

I told him hello.

He smiled at me. "Yes, yes, yes," he said, "I know exactly how it is to have to sit in school all day and have to hold your water. I am quite used to the habits of young men. I was president of a liberal arts college in Michigan." He noticed that I was wearing my cutoffs, my usual beachcombing outfit, so he slapped his thighs and set them to shimmying like two pots of vanilla yogurt. "I see you're ready. Let's get going. The tide's halfway out already, and as they say, 'Time and tide wait for no man.' Tide was better a few hours ago. I found a couple of real beauties. Locked them in the glove compartment of my car."

I walked with him to the beach, and we began our hunt. He wasn't bending over for falsies very much anymore. Each time he bent over, he yelled, "Got one!" and then he'd hold it up in the air and wouldn't put it in his bag until I nodded or said something or both. President Bob ended up with about twenty teeth, one vertebra bone, and of the twenty, one was a real trophy, an inch long, heavy root and the whole edge serrated with nothing worn away. A real trophy.

I found eight. Three of them were medium, four of them were itty-bitty and one had the tip crushed off.

I got up early the next day and checked the tide; it was just starting out. Good, I thought. I crossed the road and ran out onto the beach, rolling up my pajama bottoms as I walked along. The tide was just right; it was leaving long saw-tooth edges of coquina, and I managed to collect eight decent-sized teeth and one right-good-sized one before I ran back home and hosed off my feet and got dressed for school. I stuffed my collection into the pockets of my cutoffs. I had to skip breakfast, a fact that didn't particularly annoy me until about eleven o'clock. That afternoon, for every two times President Bob stooped down and yelled "Got one!" I did it three times.

On Friday I didn't want to skip breakfast again, and

my mother for sure didn't want me to, so President Bob was way ahead.

On Saturday I got up before dawn and dressed and sat on our dock until I saw the first thin line of dawn. Dawn coming over the intracoastal is like watching someone draw up a Venetian blind. On a clear day the sky lifts slowly and evenly, and it makes a guy feel more than okay to see it happen. But on that Saturday, I sat on the dock just long enough to make sure that daylight was to the east of me before I crossed the highway and began heading north. Shoot! I think that if the Lord had done some skywriting that morning, I wouldn't have taken the time to read it, even if it was in English.

Finally, I climbed to the top of a tall dune and walked up one and down another. I was heading for a place between the dunes about a mile to the north. I knew that during spring, when the moon was new, there was a tidewater between two of the dunes. Sharks' teeth got trapped in it, and sometimes Mom and I would go there if there was a special size she was looking for to finish an arrangement. You had to dig down into the coquina, and it wasn't much fun finding sharks' teeth this way instead of sauntering along the beach and happening to find them. But sometimes it was necessary.

I dug.

I dug and I dug and I dug.

I put all my findings into a clam shell that I found, and I dug, and I dug, and I dug. I felt the sun hot on my back, and I still dug. I had my back to the ocean and my face to the ground and for all I knew there was no sky and no sea and no sand and no colors. There was nothing, nothing, and nothing except black, and that black was the black of fossil teeth.

I had filled the clam shell before I stopped digging. I sorted the teeth and put the best ones—there were fourteen of them—in my right side pocket—the one with a button—and I put all the smaller ones in my back pocket and started back toward home, walking along the strand. I figured that I had a good head start on the day and on President Bob. I would pepper my regular findings with the ones I had just dug up. I'd mix the little ones in with the fourteen big ones. But, I decided, smiling to myself, I'd have a run of about eight big ones in a row just to see what he would do.

My back felt that it was near to burning up, and I looked toward the ocean, and it looked powerful good. The morning ocean in the spring can be as blue as the phony color they paint it on a geography book map. Sometimes there are dark patches in it, and the gulls sweep down on top of the dark spots. I decided that I needed to take a dip in that ocean. I half expected a cloud of steam to rise up off my back. I forgot about time and tide and sharks' teeth and ducked under the waves and licked the salt off my lips as I came back up.

I was feeling pretty good, ready to face President Bob and the world, and then I checked my pockets and found that about half the supply from my back pocket had tumbled out, and I had lost two big ones. I was pretty upset about that, so I slowed down on my walk back home. I crouched down and picked up shell pieces, something I thought that I had outgrown, but that is about how anxious I was not to let anything get by me. I found a couple of medium-sized ones and put them in my back pocket and began a more normal walk when my trained eye saw a small tooth right at the tide line.

I reached down to pick it up, figuring that, if nothing

else, it would add bulk to my collection the way they add cereal to hot dog meat. I didn't have any idea how many baby teeth I had lost out of my back pocket.

When I reached down to pick up that little tooth, it didn't come up immediately, and I began to think that maybe it was the tip of a really big one. I stooped down and carefully scraped away the wet sand and saw that there were several teeth together. The tide was rushing back up to where I was, so I laid my hand flat down on the ground and shoveled up a whole fistful of wet, cool sand.

I walked back to the dune and gently scraped away the sand with the forefinger of my other hand, and then I saw what I had.

There were several teeth, and they were attached to a piece of bone, a piece of jawbone. There was a space between the third tooth and the fourth, and the smallest tooth, the one on the end that I had first seen, was attached to the jawbone by only a thin edge.

I had never seen such a trophy. I felt that the spirit of the Lord had come mightily upon me, like Samson. Except that I had the jawbone of a shark and not the jawbone of an ass. And I wanted to smite only one president, not a thousand Philistines.

I didn't run the rest of the way home. I was too careful for that. I walked, holding that trophy in my hand, making certain that it didn't dry out before I could see if the weak tooth was fossilized onto the bone.

I called to Mom when I came into the house and when she appeared at the door to the screened porch, I uncurled my fingers one by one until the whole bone and all four of the teeth were showing. I watched Mom's face, and it was like watching the dawn I had missed.

"Ah, Ned," she said, "it is the Nobel Prize of trophies." We walked into the kitchen. She wet a good wad of paper towels and lifted the jawbone carefully from my hand and put it down on that pad of paper. And then we sat down at the kitchen table and I told her about how I found it, and I told it all to her in detail. Dad came in and Mom asked me to tell him, and I did and she listened just as hard the second time.

We ate our breakfast, and afterwards, we wet the paper towels again and moved the trophy onto a plastic place mat on the kitchen table. Mom looked at it through the magnifying glass and then handed me the glass so that I could look at it too.

While we were studying it hard like that, President Bob came to the screen door and said, "Knock, knock."

Mom nodded at me, her way of letting me know that I was supposed to invite him on in.

"Well, well," he said. "Are we ready for today's treasure hunt?"

"I guess so," I said, as easy as you please, moving a little to the left so that he could catch a glimpse of what Mom and I were looking at.

He gave it a glance and then another one right quick.

Mom and I looked at each other as he came closer and closer to the table. He studied that trophy from his full height and from behind a chair. Next thing, he moved in front of the chair. And next after that he sat down in the chair. And then, not taking his eyes off that trophy, he held his hand out for the magnifying glass and Mom took it from me and gave it to him.

The whole time he did this, I watched his face. His eyes squinched up and his jaw dropped open and his nostrils flared. It was like watching a minimovie called *Jealousy and Greed.*

I could feel myself smiling. "Found it this morning," I said.

Then I didn't say anything anymore. And I stopped smiling.

I thought about his face, and that made me think about mine. If his face was a movie called *Jealousy and Greed,* I didn't like the words I could put to mine.

I gently pushed the place mat closer to President Bob. "Look at it," I said. "Look at it good." I waited until his eyes were level with mine. "It's for you," I said. "It's a present from me."

"Why, thank you, boy," he said.

"Name's Ned," I answered, as I walked around to the other side of the table and emptied my pockets. "Do you think we can make something pretty out of these?" I asked Mom.

She gave me a Nobel Prize of a smile for an answer. President Bob didn't even notice, he was so busy examining the jawbone with which he had been smitten.

Langston Hughes, "Thank You, Ma'am"

Mrs. Luella Bates Washington Jones. The name itself, spoken with a sense of dignity and self-respect, is a formidable one. Similarly formidable for Roger (whose unsuccessful attempt at purse snatching has put him "in contact" with Mrs. Jones) is figuring her out. For him the matter is clear: he has failed and now faces a familiar lecture, at best, or jail, at the worst. Or, if he can free himself from her grasp, he can run. But a person like Mrs. Luella Bates Washington Jones does not fit easily into the categories developed by Roger to get by in his world, so the night offers him some perplexing moments. Mrs. Jones's approach, although unfamiliar to Roger, meets his needs in a way the expected responses would not.

Thank You, Ma'am

by Langston Hughes

SHE WAS A large woman with a large purse that had everything in it but a hammer and nails. It had a long strap, and she carried it slung across her shoulder. It was about eleven o'clock at night, dark, and she was walking alone, when a boy ran up behind her and tried to snatch her purse. The strap broke with the sudden single tug the boy gave it from behind. But the boy's weight and the weight of the purse combined caused him to lose his balance. Instead of taking off full blast as he had hoped, the boy fell on his back on the sidewalk and his legs flew up. The large woman simply turned around and kicked him right square in his blue-jeaned sitter. Then she reached down, picked the boy up by his shirt front, and shook him until his teeth rattled.

After that the woman said, "Pick up my pocketbook, boy, and give it here."

She still held him tightly. But she bent down enough to permit him to stoop and pick up her purse. Then she said, "Now ain't you ashamed of yourself?"

Firmly gripped by his shirt front, the boy said, "Yes'm."

The woman said, "What did you want to do it for?"

The boy said, "I didn't aim to."

She said, "You a lie!"

By that time two or three people passed, stopped, turned to look, and some stood watching.

"If I turn you loose, will you run?" asked the woman.

"Yes'm," said the boy.

"Then I won't turn you loose," said the woman. She did not release him.

"Lady, I'm sorry," whispered the boy.

"Um-hum! Your face is dirty. I got a great mind to wash your face for you. Ain't you got nobody home to tell you to wash your face?"

"No'm," said the boy.

"Then it will get washed this evening," said the large woman, starting up the street, dragging the frightened boy behind her.

He looked as if he were fourteen or fifteen, frail and willow-wild, in tennis shoes and blue jeans.

The woman said, "You ought to be my son. I would teach you right from wrong. Least I can do right now is to wash your face. Are you hungry?"

"No'm," said the being-dragged boy. "I just want you to turn me loose."

"Was I bothering *you* when I turned that corner?" asked the woman.

"No'm."

"But you put yourself in contact with *me,*" said the woman. "If you think that that contact is not going to last awhile, you got another thought coming. When I get through with you, sir, you are going to remember Mrs. Luella Bates Washington Jones."

Sweat popped out on the boy's face and he began to struggle. Mrs. Jones stopped, jerked him around in front of her, put a half nelson about his neck, and continued to drag him up the street. When she got to her door, she dragged the boy inside, down a hall, and into a large kitchenette-furnished room at the rear of the house. She switched on the light and left the door open. The boy could hear other roomers laughing and talking in the large house. Some of their doors were open, too, so he knew he and the woman were not alone. The woman still had him by the neck in the middle of her room.

She said, "What is your name?"

"Roger," answered the boy.

"Then, Roger, you go to that sink and wash your face," said the woman, whereupon she turned him loose —at last. Roger looked at the door—looked at the woman—looked at the door—*and went to the sink.*

"Let the water run until it gets warm," she said. "Here's a clean towel."

"You gonna take me to jail?" asked the boy, bending over the sink.

"Not with that face, I would not take you nowhere," said the woman. "Here I am trying to get home to cook me a bite to eat, and you snatch my pocketbook! Maybe you ain't been to your supper either, late as it be. Have you?"

"There's nobody home at my house," said the boy.

"Then we'll eat," said the woman. "I believe you're hungry—or been hungry—to try to snatch my pocketbook!"

"I want a pair of blue suede shoes," said the boy.

"Well, you didn't have to snatch *my* pocketbook to get some suede shoes," said Mrs. Luella Bates Washington Jones. "You could of asked me."

"Ma'am?"

The water dripping from his face, the boy looked at her. There was a long pause. A very long pause. After he had dried his face and not knowing what else to do, dried it again, the boy turned around, wondering what next. The door was open. He could make a dash for it down the hall. He could run, run, run, *run!*

The woman was sitting on the day bed. After a while she said, "I were young once and I wanted things I could not get."

There was another long pause. The boy's mouth opened. Then he frowned, not knowing he frowned.

The woman said, "Um-hum! You thought I was going to say *but,* didn't you? You thought I was going to say, *but I didn't snatch people's pocketbooks.* Well, I wasn't going to say that." Pause. Silence. "I have done things, too, which I would not tell you, son—neither tell God, if He didn't already know. Everybody's got something in common. So you set down while I fix us something to eat. You might run that comb through your hair so you will look presentable."

In another corner of the room behind a screen was a gas plate and an icebox. Mrs. Jones got up and went behind the screen. The woman did not watch the boy to see if he was going to run now, nor did she watch her purse, which she left behind her on the day bed. But the boy took care to sit on the far side of the room, away from the purse, where he thought she could easily see him out of the corner of her eye if she wanted to. He did not trust the woman *not* to trust him. And he did not want to be mistrusted now.

"Do you need somebody to go to the store," asked the boy, "maybe to get some milk or something?"

"Don't believe I do," said the woman, "unless you just want sweet milk yourself. I was going to make cocoa out of this canned milk I got here."

"That will be fine," said the boy.

She heated some lima beans and ham she had in the icebox, made the cocoa, and set the table. The woman did not ask the boy anything about where he lived, or his folks, or anything else that would embarrass him. Instead, as they ate, she told him about her job in a hotel beauty shop that stayed open late, what the work was like, and how all kinds of women came in and out, blondes, redheads, and Spanish. Then she cut him a half of her ten-cent cake.

"Eat some more, son," she said.

When they were finished eating, she got up and said, "Now here, take this ten dollars and buy yourself some blue suede shoes. And next time, do not make the mistake of latching onto *my* pocketbook *nor nobody else's*—because shoes got by devilish ways will burn your feet. I got to get my rest now. But from here on in, son, I hope you will behave yourself."

She led him down the hall to the front door and opened it. "Good night! Behave yourself, boy!" she said, looking out into the street as he went down the steps.

The boy wanted to say something other than, "Thank you, ma'am," to Mrs. Luella Bates Washington Jones, but although his lips moved, he couldn't even say that as he turned at the foot of the barren stoop and looked up at the large woman in the door. Then she shut the door.

Katherine Paterson, "Woodrow Kennington Works Practically a Miracle"

Eleven-year-old Woodrow Kennington, "stoopid Whoodrow" to his sister Sara Jane, has a problem. It's not just that Sara Jane has achieved juvenile-delinquent status in her five short years, or that she recently destroyed a "practically priceless" stamp collection, or that she refuses to acknowledge their newborn brother. That sort of behavior Woodrow expects; but her shift in television habits to *The One True Word* starring Brother Austin Barnes ushers in a new era of prayers and food-chilling blessings. That stage is followed by an even more disturbing one when her God fails to deliver. Remember, though, that this is Woodrow's story, not Sara Jane's, and you will see not only his misery, but also his desire to manage the situation skillfully and maturely as well as his growing understanding of his sister's needs. You will find yourself like his friend Ralph: always amused, occasionally required to get "properly serious," and ultimately impressed with Woodrow's work that Christmas Eve.

Woodrow Kennington Works
Practically a Miracle

by Katherine Paterson

"THE FIRST THING I see when I open the door is Sara Jane lying on the rug with my stamp collection all over the place." Woodrow was sitting on the curb in front of his house trying to explain the tragic events of the past hour to his friend Ralph. "My *stamp* collection!"

Ralph was doing his best to sound sympathetic. "Geez," he said.

"I start screaming like an idiot, 'What the hell you think you're doing?' She says—you know how she sticks up her eyebrow—only five-year-old I ever heard of could poke up one eyebrow—she says, cool as can be, 'Hi, Whoodrow.' Blowing my name out like birthday candles. 'Hi, Whoodrow. I'm playing post office.' *Post office!*" Woodrow bent over in pain. "Post office with practically priceless stamps I inherited from my grandfather. I was practically crying out loud. 'Why? Why?'" Woodrow spread out both arms, imitating himself. "'Why are you playing post office with my stamps?'"

"And she says?"

"She says—get this—she says, 'Don't be stoopid, Whoodrow. You gotta have stamps to play post office.'"

"Oh, yeah?" Ralph grinned and poked him in the ribs with an elbow. "Just ask Jennifer Leonard."

"Shut up, Ralph. You haven't even heard the worst part yet."

Ralph tried to get properly serious. "There's a worst part?"

"About this time my mother comes rushing in, in a bathrobe. It is three thirty in the afternoon. My sister has destroyed an entire fortune in rare stamps while my mother has been taking a nap."

"Yeah?"

"The *reason* she has been taking a nap and let my juvenile-delinquent sister run wild—she takes me off to the den and shuts the door to tell me this goody—the reason she laid down and took her eye off Sara Jane 'for one minute' is that she is pregnant."

"Yeah?"

"My mother is thirty-eight years old."

"So?"

"Ralph, she is too old already to handle Sara Jane."

At about eight that evening Ralph called. After the usual questions about homework had been taken care of, he said, "You know, I been thinking about what you told me. I don't think you should be too upset."

"Ralph! That was a practically priceless stamp collection!"

"No, I don't mean about the stamps. I mean about becoming a brother again. Wood, face it. You got no place to go but up, man. When this next kid is five, you're sixteen. Sixteen. You know what a sixteen-year-old guy looks like to a five-year-old? Geez. This kid is liable to worship you."

It was not the worst idea Ralph had ever had. In fact, the more Woodrow thought about it, the better it sounded. His mother was surprised and delighted when he started going out of his way to help her. She began to treat him more and more like an adult. She even asked him to try to get Sara Jane to accept the idea of a new baby.

This was no small problem. Sara Jane had expressed neither excitement nor resentment when they told her. She simply pretended that she hadn't heard. Once when he was baby-sitting, Woodrow tried very hard to explain the whole situation to her. He even threw in a few interesting facts of life as a bonus.

"Don't be stoopid, Whoodrow." She never mentioned the subject again, or even seemed to hear others mention it, until the day she found Woodrow and his mother putting together the old baby bed in her room.

She marched in, hands on hips. "Get this junk outta my room."

"Sara Jane, it's for the baby." Mother was superpatient. "You remember, I talked to you yesterday . . ."

"I'm not having no baby."

"We're all having a baby, Sara Jane."

"Not me."

"Okay. *I'm* having a baby, but . . ."

"Then put this junk in your own room."

"But, darling, I explained, there's no place. . . ."

Woodrow offered on the spot to take the baby into his room. His mother stalled and his father fumed, but eventually the bed, bureau, and rocking chair took the place of his racing-car setup. His father bought a screen and covered it with airline posters, but he needn't have. Woodrow was not feeling anything like a martyr. It was the chance of a lifetime. He would start this kid out right. No more Sara Janes for him.

As for Sara Jane, she would come to Woodrow's door and stand there with her hands on her hips, her eyebrow elevated, staring at the crib legs peeking out below the bottom of the screen, but she never said a word. Occasionally, though, she would sigh—a sigh as long and weary as the *whooo-oosh* of his mother's ancient percolator. It made Woodrow uneasy, but not prepared for what happened next. He wondered later if he should have been prepared. Shouldn't he have taken a cue from her strange shift in TV programs? What normal kid would move in the span of two weeks from *The Electric Company* to *Speed Racer* to, of all things, *The One True Word*, starring Brother Austin Barnes? He had really meant to ask her about it, but the switch took place in the last wild days before the baby was born, and frankly, everyone was so glad to have her quiet and occupied that they neglected to keep a proper check on what she was watching.

When his father called from the hospital at seven o'clock to tell him that he had a brother, Woodrow let out a whoop that could have been heard for blocks. It brought Sara Jane out of the den into the kitchen. "It's a boy!" Woodrow yelled at her. "A boy!"

She watched him with a very peculiar expression on her face—neither anger nor surprise, certainly not delight. Where had he seen it before? A memory of old fading pictures in the back of the Sunday School closet came to his mind—it was that same sickly sweet half smile.

Then she let him have it. "Brother Whoodrow," she said. "I saw Jesus today."

"You what?"

Her smile, if anything, got more sickly. "I said, 'I saw Jesus.' "

Surely it was that religious program she had been watching—that combined with the shock of the news he had just given her. He felt very generous, almost sorry for her, so he tried to be kindly. "So you saw Jesus, huh?"

"I was walking home from school. All alone. Nobody meets me halfway anymore. Mommy got too fat, and Mrs. Judson is too lazy." She paused to let these sad words sink in. "But Jesus loves me. Just like Brother Austin says. When Jesus saw me coming home from school, he stopped his big black car. 'Hi,' he says."

"Sara Jane, that wasn't Jesus. He never had any big black car."

"He does now."

Woodrow was beginning to feel panicky. "Did he ask you to get into the car or anything?"

"No," she said primly.

He was not about to let Sara Jane get kidnapped while his mother was in the hospital. He told Mrs. Judson, who was staying there days, that Sara Jane had to be met at the school door. Mrs. Judson read one of those newspapers that never hesitate to give all the gory details, so when he told her about the big black car, she made the trip to the kindergarten door every day, lazy or not.

In the meantime, Daniel came home. He was the greatest baby in the world, even when he cried. In fact, Woodrow's favorite time was when Daniel cried at two o'clock in the morning. His mother would fuss and apologize when she'd come in and find Woodrow awake, but then they'd talk while she fed the baby. What a warm, good feeling to be talking in the middle of the night—grown-up to grown-up. It would have been the happiest time of his life except for Sara Jane.

He may have saved her from kidnapping, but he certainly hadn't solved the real problem. He wasn't sure if he was going to be able to stand it. Sara Jane the screaming baby, he had endured. Sara Jane the unbearable brat, he had gotten more or less used to. But Sara Jane the Saint was about to do him in.

Ralph thought it was the funniest thing since Whoopee cushions, but he didn't have to live with her. She was always smiling at him and calling him Brother Whoodrow and begging him to watch *The One True Word* with her. She prayed all the time. If Mrs. Judson fussed at her, she would go into her room and fall on her knees, praying that God would forgive poor bad Mrs. Judson. It was Woodrow's job to fix breakfast for the two of them. Sara Jane would bless the food until the toast had turned to floor tile.

But even that he might have put up with had she not announced to him one morning that their parents were going to Hell.

"Shut up, Sara Jane."

"But they're lost!" she said.

"They are not lost. They're Presbyterians."

"See? They don't even know they're lost and going to Hell."

"Well, why don't you just tell them?"

"They'd laugh at me."

They would, too. He wanted to laugh himself, but he couldn't quite. Suppose his father and mother were headed for Hell and didn't even know it? Suppose he were? They were all bound for Hell while Sara Jane . . . Suddenly, as the robots would say, it did not compute. Sara Jane the Saint was pure plastic—the fake of all fakes. Instead of letting her scare him, he should be whipping her back into shape. It was up to him to get her back to normal. Normal, mind you, was never all that great, but normal he could manage.

First, he would silence *The One True Word*. Fortunately, the TV set was practically an antique, which meant all he had to do was take a couple of tubes out of the back and hide them in his bureau drawer beneath his underwear.

When Sara Jane complained to her father that the TV was broken, he hardly looked up from his newspaper. He didn't like TV anyhow, which was why he'd never bothered to get a decent set, much less color.

"Who is going to fix the TV?" she persisted.

Her father put down his paper. "Nobody has time to bother with that TV before Christmas. Besides"—he was already back behind the paper—"you watch too much TV anyway."

Woodrow found her some minutes later on her knees in the den, her hand on the cold set. "O Lord"—Woodrow wasn't sure if she was praying aloud for his benefit or God's—"O Lord, make this TV set well. The Devil broke it, but you can make it well."

"Sara Jane!" He was so shocked that he burst right into her prayer. She ignored him and kept on rocking and praying. Woodrow was not crazy about being called the Devil, but he sure as heck was not going to put the tubes back now and turn the kid into a permanent religious weirdo.

Next morning at breakfast, there were no lengthy announcements. Sara Jane just rolled her eyes up at the ceiling and said, "Okay, God. You know what you gotta do." And in answer to Woodrow's openmouthed stare, she said, "He knows if he doesn't hurry up and fix that set, I'm not going to believe in him anymore."

When he came in from school two days in a row to find

her praying over the TV set, he began to weaken. "How about me taking you Christmas shopping, Sara Jane?"

Slowly she turned and gave him her saddest face. "I guess I'm not going to believe in Christmas this year. The TV still doesn't work."

"Oh"—his voice sounded very cheery and very faky—"I wouldn't give up on Christmas just because of some old TV. Maybe it's just a broken tube or something."

"God can do anything he wants to. If he doesn't want to fix this TV, it means he doesn't want me to be his child. I guess nobody wants me to be their child."

Ralph, after he stopped laughing, suggested that Woodrow launch a campaign. It was obvious that the child felt insecure. Woodrow needed to prove to her that her family really loved her. Then she would be cured.

Woodrow was desperate enough to try anything, even a suggestion from Ralph. He persuaded his mother that she was not too tired to make cookies with Sara Jane, since he, Woodrow, would clean up the entire kitchen afterward. Sara Jane made twelve gorgeous gingerbread men, all scowling. Woodrow talked his father into taking Sara Jane on a special trip to see Santa Claus. She had climbed, after much urging, onto the old fellow's lap, only to ask him why his breath smelled all mediciny. Woodrow himself devoted a full Saturday morning to helping Sara Jane make a crèche out of baker's dough.

"Sara Jane." He tried not to sound too critical. "We can't use fourteen snakes in one manger scene."

"That's all I feel like making, Whoodrow. Just snakes and snakes"—she sighed—"dead snakes."

"Suppose," he said, his eyes carefully on the sheep he

was modeling, "suppose the TV would get well. Would you feel better then?"

"It's too late. God flunked already."

"Maybe he just needed a little more time, or something."

She looked him dead in the eye. "If the TV got fixed now, I'd know it was you or daddy did it. Just to shut me up. You're just scared I'm going to mess up your old Christmas. That's all you care about."

He tried to protest, but she was too close to the truth. How could he enjoy Christmas when he felt like some kind of a monster?

Christmas Eve their parents went off to church, leaving him in charge. There had been a bit of trouble earlier when Sara Jane had refused at first to hang up her stocking. "I just don't believe in Christmas anymore," she had said wearily. Their parents hadn't known whether to take her seriously or not, but Woodrow had. He whispered in her ear that if she didn't hang up her stocking that minute he was going to beat the you-know-what out of her the minute the folks walked out the door. She sighed, that long now-frequent sigh of hers, and handed him her stocking to put up.

After he had gotten her, still moaning and sighing, into bed, he sank into the big living-room chair, staring miserably at the blinking lights of the Christmas tree. The tree itself looked so fat and jolly and merry that he was close to tears when the telephone rang.

It was Ralph. He was baby-sitting, too, but he was so cheerful it made Woodrow feel murderous. "Say, there's this great movie on Channel Seven. It was practically X-rated when it first came out."

"Our TV's broken, remember?"

Ralph chortled. "I also remember, old buddy, that you can work that little miracle whenever you want to."

Woodrow slammed down the receiver. Everything always seemed simple to Ralph. When Ralph looked at his Christmas tree, he didn't have to see at its base fourteen dead snakes guarding a manger scene. If only he could fix everything as easily as he could fix that blasted TV. Well, what the heck? A practically X-rated movie was sure to take his mind off Sara Jane for a little while.

He dug the tubes out of his underwear drawer and put them back into the TV set. The old set warmed as slowly as ever, gradually filling the den with the sound of Christmas music. He reached out to switch the channel, but before he could do so, the hundred-voiced TV choir sang a line that made his fingers stop in midair.

"See him in a manger laid whom the angels praise above. . . ."

I saw Jesus today. That's what Sara Jane had said that had started this whole mess. What was so wrong, after all, with a lonesome little kid, even a bad—maybe especially a bad—little lonesome kid wanting some proof that God cared about her? It was not as if she were eleven and needed to face the facts. Maybe Ralph had an idea, after all. Maybe Woodrow could work a little miracle.

He took the hedge clipper out to the backyard and cut so much dried grass and weeds that it took him four or five trips to carry it all in. He dumped his underwear on the bed, put his pillow into the drawer, and covered it with grass. The rest of the grass and weeds he scattered across the living-room floor. He put the drawer on a footstool in front of the Christmas tree. The knobs were showing, so he turned it around. He turned off the blinking lights. The lighting had to be just so, or it wouldn't work. He tried a single candle on the end table. Better. He experimented with the music from the TV in the den until he got it just loud enough to sound sort of mysterious. Then, very carefully, his heart thumping madly against his chest, he lifted the still-sleeping Daniel from his bed, wrapped him in a crib sheet, and laid him in the drawer. When he was satisfied that everything was perfect, he wrapped his own top sheet around himself and went to get Sara Jane.

He shook her and then stepped back near the door. "Sara Jane!" He made his voice strong and slightly spooky. "Sara Jane!" She stirred in her sleep. "Sara Jane Kennington!"

Slowly Sara Jane sat up.

"Sara Jane!" She was looking around trying to figure out, perhaps, where the voice was coming from, so he hiked up his sheet and spread his arms out wide. "Arise!" he commanded. "Arise and follow me!"

Now she saw him—at least she turned and looked straight at him—but when she slid out of bed and padded toward the door, it was as though she were sleepwalking. He turned quickly and led her down the hall. Just as they got to the doorway into the living room, he stepped back and gestured for her to go ahead.

She went on for a few steps and then stopped. He watched her back. Her thin little body was shivering under her pajamas. Her head moved back and forth very slowly. She was taking the whole scene in. And it was beautiful. Even when you knew. Like that painting of the shepherds in the dark barn where the only light comes from the manger. The baby had worked his arms and legs loose from the sheet and was waving them in the air.

Above the angel music you could hear his happy bubbling noises.

"Ohh." Sara Jane let out such a long sigh that her whole body shuddered. "Ohhh." She dared a tiny step forward. "Hi, Jesus," she said.

There was something so quiet, so pure, about the way she said it that it went straight through to Woodrow's stomach. He found he was shaking all over. Why was he so cold and scared? He had fooled her, hadn't he? He ought to be feeling proud, not sick to his stomach.

Sara Jane took another step toward the baby. Now what was he supposed to do? He hadn't given any thought to what he should do *after* the miracle. Stupid. Stupid. Stupid. He reached out to stop her from going any farther and stumbled over his sheet. "Oh, hell!"

She turned around, half afraid, half puzzled. "Whoodrow?"

"Don't be scared, Sara Jane. It's just me." He disentangled himself from the sheet. "Stoopid old Whoodrow." The choir from the den launched into a series of hallelujahs. "Oh, shut up!"

Sara Jane in the candlelight might have been a little princess waking from an enchanted sleep. Finally, she cocked her head. "Is that the TV?" she asked.

"Yeah." He turned on the 150-watt reading lamp. "I fixed it."

She blinked a moment in the brightness, and then marched over to the fake manger. "That's Daniel in there."

"Yeah." He was beginning to feel hot. "I was trying to fool you." He flopped heavily to the couch. "Sara Jane, for your future information, nobody should go around trying to fake miracles. First, I broke the TV so you wouldn't be religious, and then I fixed all this junk"—he waved his arm around the room—"so you would. Go ahead. Say it. I'm stoopid."

She came over to the couch and ducked her head so she could look up into his face. "This wasn't stoopid," she said. "I liked it."

She must not understand what he was trying to say. He repeated himself. "I was the one that broke the TV set in the first place."

"Huh?"

"I couldn't stand you praying and acting good all the time."

She looked surprised. "I thought you wanted me to be good, Whoodrow. You used to hate me when I was bad."

"I never hated you. Honest."

"Well"—she sighed her old weary sigh—"Mommy and Daddy did. They wouldn't have got a new one if they liked the old one."

His shame began to shift in the direction of the old exasperation. "Sara Jane Kennington, do you think they stopped liking me when you were born? Maybe they loved me even better than before."

"Really?" He thought she was going to smile, but instead her face clouded up. "Well, I know for sure God hates me. I been so bad." Her chin began to quiver. "I know for sure God hates me."

"Sara Jane. God is crazy about you."

First her eyebrow went up; then she giggled. "You're stoopid, Whoodrow."

"Maybe so," he said. "And then again, maybe not."

When he thought about it later, Woodrow wondered if his miracle had been so fake after all. Ralph's definition of a miracle was something that no one in his right mind would believe. And Ralph, for one, could not believe that Woodrow Kennington had spent Christmas Eve raking grass off his living-room floor while listening happily to his sister sing through practically the entire "Hallelujah Chorus" accompanied by a silver-voiced choir of thousands. In fact, now that Sara Jane was back to normal, he had some trouble believing it himself.

Jill Paton Walsh, "Crossing to Salamis"

Young Aster lives a confined life—her mother considers it respectable—in the Greek city-state of Athens. Aster tells us she can "count on the fingers of one hand" her ventures out of the house; she spends her time in the women's room, which looks out onto a courtyard and the distant Acropolis but not onto a single public street. However, the life that Aster—and all of Athens, for that matter—have known is threatened by invading Persians in 480 B.C. Aster's mother reluctantly joins the Athenians making the crossing to the nearby island of Salamis, where Aster is freed from her confinement. She even feels a "wild surge of joy" that her life, already utterly changed, cannot return to the old pattern as she watches smoke rise from the city, set ablaze by the Persians. As the decisive naval battle between the Greeks and the Persians off Salamis nears, Aster risks public disgrace in a courageous effort to protect her people from betrayal. Aster, the first-person narrator, tells her own story of moving from stifling confinement to wide-ranging freedom, from inactivity to bold action, from isolation to involvement.

Crossing to Salamis
by Jill Paton Walsh

IF ONLY I had known how completely my city would be destroyed! If only I had known that I would live to see it burned and overthrown and smashed to rubble so thoroughly that folk who had lived in a street all their lives would be unable to discern among the ruins the line that street had taken! If I *had* known, I would have looked keenly and lovingly at the view from the women's room in our house, though from what I can remember there was little enough to see.

My mother and I, and Phryne, my nurse, spent all day in that upper room, spinning wool and weaving on two huge looms. And from our high window we could see below us an undulating furrowed field of roof tiles, as brown and red as the earth of Attica, stretching to the temple-crowned crag of the Acropolis. We looked down into our own tiny courtyard, but not into a single street; in the whole of Athens the only movements we could see were the distant figures of people moving on the Acropolis, or mounting its zigzag path. These people my mother did not mind seeing—though I could never tell whether it was because they were so far off that they seemed as small as the tiny figures painted on pottery, or because of their holy purpose in visiting the temples, that they passed as a respectable sight for a virtuous woman.

Lysia, our slave girl, worked among the empty rooms below, making bread, feeding the chickens in the yard, giving scraps to my darling pets, my Goose and my Hare. She was the one who went to the market to buy and sell for us. My mother never went out, though very occasionally some old friend of hers would come to visit us. While Nikias, my brother, was at home he brought news about horses, and ships, and votes in the Assembly; but when he was away the only news was brought by Mother's friends, and it was all about sickness and babies, deaths and marriages. Without the reports Lysia brought back of gossip in the markets, we would have been the most ignorant family in Athens.

And I, Aster, I, too, never went out; I could count on the fingers of one hand the times I had passed through the house door into the street. Once I went to the theater, when the citizens' fund paid for our seats. Once I wore white, and gold in my hair, and walked among the maidens in the festival procession for Athena. And the only other place I had ever been to was to Marathon, to lay garlands on the green mound among the olive trees that covers the brave dead who fell driving the Persians back from our shores.

And yet the word *Marathon* does not bring the green tomb to my mind, or the soft sunny day on which we went there, but instead brings up in my mind's eye the stale familiar view into the courtyard from the women's room suddenly blazing, suddenly flashing with golden light, so that I blinked, dazzled, as I looked down from the arms of Phryne, who was holding me up to see. When I asked Phryne about that she cried and told me I was remembering the sunlight on my father's brazen armor, when he kissed my mother good-bye below the window, the day the men went out to Marathon. But other than that blinding gleam, I cannot remember him. Very few Athenians were killed in that great victory—but my father was one of them.

My brother was only eight when my father died. All my father's wealth was held in trust by my uncle, and he wanted my mother to go home to her own family, and be married again. When she refused, preferring to stay here with us, he would give us nothing. We have lived on the sale of our fine spinning and the weaving at which my mother is so adept. All the slaves were sold except Lysia. As for Phryne, she is not a slave but a free woman from Sparta, employed by my father to care for us, because it is said Spartan women make the best nurses. She has not been paid an obol since my father died, and could go home at any time, but she stays. When we were children, Nikias and I, we used to think she stayed because she was ashamed to go home. For the Spartans had come so late to Marathon that the battle was won and the enemy fled away before they got there; but now I think she stays because she likes my mother. There is nothing else to keep her, we live so poorly. She says herself that she stays because Nikias promised to buy her a golden brooch the day he is enrolled as a citizen, and gets back my father's estate.

A golden brooch for Phryne; our little farm by the shore to go to in summer, away from the hot City; freedom from the endless work of the loom for my mother, money enough for my brother to live respectably, and go to the Assembly every day, and a dowry to marry me, plainly, but decently—I am fourteen already—all this had Nikias promised us and himself the day he became a citizen. How eagerly we waited for that day!

I, especially, I thought of nothing else. I hardly listened to news about anything else. If the Persians were on the march again, and all Greece was in arms to fend them off—why, Athens alone had defeated the Persians

when they came before. I knew Nikias would have to go
as an ephebe—to train as a soldier, as soon as his longed-
for birthday came—but still I did not see that the Persians had anything to do with us. The whole world had
nothing to do with us, spinning, and weaving, and talking
to Goose and Hare.

Only when Nikias kissed me good-bye did I realize.
"No, little one," he said, stooping to kiss me at the door.
"I can't come back soon. The City will give me bronze
armor, because I am one of the sons of the fallen. And I
shall put it on, and march away, with the army, to try to
stop the Persians in the north." I wept bitterly, not only
because of his words, but because of his bright eyes, and
springy step. I knew he *wanted* to go!

"You wouldn't want the Persians to come and burn
Athens, would you, pet?" he said. "Don't worry about
me, they'll train me on the march."

"And must we still be poor till you come home again?"
I wailed.

"Mother has letters of authority," he said, frowning. "I
hope it will be all right."

"Think of yourself and Athens, son," said my mother.
"Not of us. The gods protect you." But the moment he
had gone she wept as bitterly as I.

It was only a day or so later that my uncle came to visit
us. He brought his wife with him, maybe from propriety,
maybe as a witness. My mother received them behind
closed doors, but I just caught Phryne's eye, and we crept
up to the keyhole, and overheard. After all, what was
said was likely to concern us too.

"I have received instructions from Nikias," my uncle
was saying, "about handing over my brother's property

at once, and to you, since he is away. I have come to tell you that this is an impossible time for such a request. It will have to wait, like everything else."

"I know nothing about the time," said my mother— how coldly!—"that you should be prevented from doing your duty by us."

"The Persians are coming!" said my uncle. "You know that."

"The Persians have been coming ever since Marathon, to take their revenge," said my mother. "If you wait till there is no talk of the Persians coming, Nikias will never inherit without a lawsuit."

"But it's not just talk, Myro dear!" cried my uncle's wife. "If only it were! But it pleases you always to be difficult. And do you care nothing for that terrible oracle?"

"This is how things stand," said my uncle. "The army has already fallen back from northern Greece. The Spartans are holding the narrow pass at Thermopylae. Our fleet is nearby. Should the Persians force the pass they will be in Athens in three days. The Assembly has decided to evacuate the City, if need be, and I fear there will be need. So I am busy now, embarking my family and servants for Troezen, in good time. You can come with us if you wish. As for property, nothing could be more ridiculous than handing it over now—if the Persians come, there will be nothing to hand over."

"And then again," said my mother bitterly, "perhaps Nikias will not survive to take it from you."

"That, too, it must be faced, is a possibility," said my uncle. "This will be no skirmish, like Marathon. Xerxes the King himself is coming, with so great an army that they drink the rivers dry in their passing, and with innumerable ships. We are all at risk."

"Come with us, Myro," said my uncle's wife. "I have made sure there is room for two in our party."

"There are four in my household," said my mother.

"Your people won't be alone in fending for themselves; people all over the City are leaving their slaves."

"How disgraceful," said my mother, and with that my relations left.

My mother put a long cloak over her tunic, and went with Phryne to visit a childhood friend of hers, a priestess on the Acropolis. I was left alone, feeling scared, to talk to Lysia.

"The Persians are really coming, this time," I told her.

"Old news," she said, punching the ball of dough.

"How can you be so calm!" I wailed.

"We still need bread, don't we?" she said. "And what of it, anyway? Do the Persians treat slaves worse than the Athenians do?"

"But, Lysia, you don't mind being a slave, do you?" I asked, astonished. "And Nikias will give you your freedom as soon as we can afford it."

"If the Persians don't get here first!" said Lysia. "Now, just get out of my way, young mistress, or there really won't be any bread today."

When my mother returned she called us all together, and the four of us sat in solemn conference, like men. "It is true there had been a bad oracle from Delphi," said my mother. "It told the Athenians to flee, and that safety would lie only in their wooden walls. And some think that means the Acropolis will be safe, because the old men can remember a time when it had a wooden wall around it; but a man called Themistocles has persuaded most people that it means we should trust to our ships; that the people must go to Salamis, and the men must fight the barbarian at sea."

"Good," said Phryne calmly. "Then we must make ready. We shall need blankets . . ."

"No," said my mother. "Who is this Themistocles? He is a nobody—an upstart. His mother was not even an Athenian. Of course he favors ships—fox that he is, any rabble can row ships. We must wait to see what the noble families in the City do—those who provide fighting men. If they will go off on a wild-goose chase to Salamis, well. Otherwise we, too, will go to the Acropolis and trust the gods. They are building a new wooden wall around it. And anyway, the Spartans and Leonidas their king are holding the pass. The Persians may never come."

"If we must go, Myro," said Phryne—and I had never heard her use my mother's name before—"there is much to be said for going soon."

"We are not rabble," said my mother, "and we will not behave like it."

So we just stayed. But I saw Phryne put together rolls of good cloth, some rope, a jar of pitch, a sack of meal, a jar of oil, and a jar of olives, and stack them all ready at the door.

The whole world knows how the Spartans were betrayed at Thermopylae. How they were betrayed and surrounded, and all killed, and the Persian hordes came flooding into Attica. We heard no news, but we guessed what had happened, from the running and wailing in the streets around us, from cries and shouts, and noise, from horses' hooves and rumbling cartwheels. This uproar began in the afternoon, and continued far into the night.

"We would get trampled to death if we went now,"

said my mother, contemptuously. But for the first time in my life, I wondered if she was right.

At dawn we could see great crowds heaving bundles and weapons up to the Acropolis. We could see the wooden fence around it, hastily made. My mother stood at her high window and looked. And she and Phryne began to quarrel.

". . . a Spartan woman would be ashamed!" Phryne's raised voice reached me where I sat in the courtyard, fondling Hare's silken coat. "Making excuse after excuse! The truth is you are afraid—afraid of so small a thing as a journey to the nearest island! All right, my dear, do you think I don't know? Haven't I lived here long enough to know? You have never been so much as a tenth the distance in your life—the way you people live, all shut up in houses, as though the gods had meant even fresh air only for men! But in Sparta women survive an active life . . . no harm comes to us. How I wish you could see . . ."

"Oh, gods, Phryne, don't start on all that again!" cried my mother. "So in Sparta you can exercise naked among men and not lose your reputation. I have heard you before! But you can't do that here. Do you think I wouldn't enjoy going about more? More talk to my neighbors? But we are without friends and without money—and I have suffered all these years because, come what may, I will preserve the only thing we do have, an impeccable reputation, an unblemished claim to be citizens. Just let people start to talk about me as a loose woman, and someone will dispute my children's rights—and what does Nikias have if that happens, or how would we marry my poor Aster with the least breath of scandal about us? All very well for you to talk . . ."

"You poor stupid thickhead!" cried Phryne. "Will it be

better if she is outraged by the Persians?" Then there was
the sound of my mother weeping. And the noise outside,
the sound of people trekking through the streets, still
continued.

When the sun was past its height that day, I said a
kind farewell to Goose and Hare. I would not have them
left caged up in our yard, to fall captive with no chance
to run away. I had made up my mind. So I boldly got up,
and unbolted the street door, and opened it. Hare lol-
loped out straightaway, but silly Goose wouldn't go, and
I chased her, and she gobbled and flapped her wings, and
made a noise. The noise brought my mother and Phryne
down into the yard to see what was amiss. And as they
stood looking through the door, and as I chased Goose
out through it, we heard singing. Young men's voices,
robustly singing together, and many footfalls—the light-
sandaled footfalls of young men.

We all three stood stock-still and watched them go by.
They were swinging jingling bridles in their hands, and
laughing together. My mother called Lysia, and told her
to run after them, and find out, if she could, what they
were doing.

"Why?" I asked. "Why does it matter?" And my
mother said one of them was Kimon, son of Miltiades,
who had been our leader at Marathon. No family in the
whole City was more noble than his. And in a moment
Lysia was back, saying they had told her they were going
to dedicate their bridles in the temple of Athene. I imagined the bright straps with their gilded mountings hanging on the temple walls, among the swords left by old
soldiers, the crutches left by those who could walk again,
the dolls left by girls getting married on the morrow. And
even I—though I am slow at such things—saw that the

young men meant they were done with horses—done with fighting in the old way.

". . . and then," Lysia was saying, "they will go and enlist on the ships!"

My mother said, "If Kimon will follow Themistocles so will we. How soon can we be ready?"

"At once," said Phryne, pointing to the things she had made ready. "But put on your thickest mantle."

At the door my mother stopped. "Nikias has no home to come back to," she said, swaying. "He will never find us. . . ." Her voice was thin and distant. Phryne grabbed hold of her in time to stop her falling, and laid her gently down, and I ran for water. But my mother's forehead was burning hot, and we knew really that she was not going to be able to walk.

"A good night's sleep to calm her spirits," said Phryne when she and Lysia had carried my mother to her bed, "and we'll go in the morning."

Twice that night I woke. I could still hear the noise of the departing people far and wide around me. But at daybreak what woke me was silence; the sound of the people going had ceased.

Lysia lit a fire to cook a little gruel to keep my mother's strength up, and Phryne led her gently down to sit in the sun while it was made. But no sooner had Lysia lit a fire, and the smoke begun drifting upward through the chimney hole, than there came a thunderous beating on our door—crash, crash, and it was smashed down from outside. In strode a young man all in bronze, all clad in gleams of sunlight off his metal limbs. Flashing and loud he called out, "Is anyone here? Who is still here?"

Then he saw my mother. "Madam, you must be gone," he said.

"Yes," she said, and stood up. He saw her sway.

"You are almost too late," he said. "Come, you must borrow my horse." He took her by the hand, as though she were his own mother, and led her into the street. And there he put his bronze arms around her, and lifted her onto his horse. Phryne picked up one bundle, and Lysia another, and the stranger took my hand in his left hand, and his bridle in his right, and led us down through the streets away from the Acropolis, a way I had never been before. As for the impropriety of it, my mother said never a word.

And so we came out of the City and down to the shore. I had never before been to the margin of the sea. At the tomb at Marathon, I had seen it far off, a blue hazy distance, but here it was at my feet. It was all sunshot with nets of light. The waves were like the curly edge of a green glass bottle I had once out of Egypt, and moved endlessly shushing and whispering and chuckling on the bright sand. And oh, how wide it was! It lay like shining silk spread out before us, scattered with glints of silver, like floating stars, so far, so far! All the way to that lilac shadow rising from the southern horizon that the young soldier said was Salamis, that famous island where we might be safe.

"You see," he said, "it is a narrow channel. Not far to go."

Not far! I had never seen a prospect of such distance before in all my life. But the boats being rowed away full of people seemed steady enough in the water, and I was not afraid. I trailed my fingers in the water and licked my fingers, to find if the sea was indeed, as Nikias had told me, salt. We were almost the last away, and behind us there were dogs barking, and a few distracted people crying. There was a moment halfway across when both the shore behind us and the shore ahead seemed melted into distant shadow, like dreams.

"We shall never see Athens again," said my mother.

"That's a gloomy saying, my friend," said an old man in a rough cloak. "Have courage."

"Never again as it was," said my mother.

"Not as it was," he said, and I saw he was letting fall silent tears.

At last the boat grounded upon the beach and we got out and waded ashore with our hems and feet wet. And there we all were, on Salamis.

The gods be thanked Phryne knew what to do. Most of the Athenians were milling about on a small plain by the shore, near the little town of Salamis. Phryne said crisply that there would be sickness within a week in a camp on such low land; she took us southward along the shore, carrying our things, till we found a remote rocky hillock rising above the beach, with a stretch of sloping rough grass around it. A little stream of fresh water bubbled from a spring among these rocks, and there was an outcrop of gray stone making an overhang just above it. Here Phryne made us a tent, stretching out lengths of our cloth between the rocks and the forked branch of a stunted bush, and sealing the joins with pitch to keep the rain out.

All the while my mother sat exhausted and dazed, leaning against the rock and saying nothing. I, too, was tired, for cutting thyme for beds, and bringing stones to build a hearth, was heavy work compared to spinning, but it was a lovely game. I was as pleased with Phryne as if she had made me another dollhouse, like the one she made once for Goose and Hare to walk in and out of.

I was falling asleep as I ate that night. We could see Athenian fires all over the plain to the north of us; we could hear a murmur of distant voices in the dark, and the strange dreamlike incantation of the waves on the shore. And it was only when I crept to my bed that astonishment gripped me. I was amazed at the lack of quiet—the sounds of the night, the crackling of the prickly sweet-smelling branches beneath us, the flapping of the flimsy tent on the cool night air. I was amazed at the lack of darkness—the glow of embers on the hearth at the tent door, and the brilliant stars in a triangle of sky. I was astonished at our lack of safety—no walls, no door to shut, no bolts, only enough wool to make us a cloak apiece, and the goodwill of the gods. In the midst of my astonishment I fell asleep.

A bright dawn woke me. My astonishment continued. I had not been acquainted with the sun until he rose high enough to shine down into our courtyard; I had not till then seen the morning glory of the sun in a wide-open place, coming low and sideways, and filling the whole liquid strait of Salamis with pale molten gold. And all day long I could watch the changing shadows on the blue water, and the lilac-gray mountainside, and feel the little playful gusts of the unconfined open air.

There was plenty to do on Salamis. There was coming and going among the citizens—we were not allowed to go where the men were camped in arms—people finding old friends, walking the beach in groups, talking and lamenting. My mother sat always near our tent, but people came to see her, women, and even men too old to fight, friends of my father's who came to offer help or talk of the old days. There were pedagogues on the island, and soon lessons were arranged for the boys, and nobody minded if the girls came and sat on the outside of the circle and listened too. And we could run, and skip, and throw ball all day, and even learn to swim in the clear cold water. My skin began to turn brown like a boy's; my cheeks to glow warm when I ran; I could run farther and faster every day.

When Mother was not looking Phryne showed me how to gird up my tunic, to leave my legs free of the clinging cloth, and thus we went scrambling up the hillside in search of birds' eggs, and likely places to set traps for hares. Nobody frowned at Phryne now for having Spartan ways, and teaching them to me. On Salamis there were only two rules for the children—not to worry the adults, and to return to our family fires well before night.

I cried long and bitterly the first time Phryne's little twig-trap caught a hare—but I ate it all the same. Once she and I climbed alone to the top of the tallest hill on the island, and from there we saw the sea shining all around us, silk pale blue, and scattered with shadow islands. And we could see the mainland to the south—mountain upon mountain, fainter and fainter, receding far away—I had not known the whole world was so wide!

"Where is Sparta?" I asked Phryne. "Which of those mountains is Taygetos?" But she said it was much farther than we could see. And all this the Persians would take from us. I had not known how much we had to lose.

Then, on our way down again, we saw the column of smoke rising from the Athenian Acropolis. The City itself could be seen from Salamis only in the clearest light—a tiny gleam of white in the hazy outlines of home—but the smoke towered upward, swelling and spreading, thick and black, fouling the sky, and slowly seeping toward us on the still air. Phryne stopped a moment, and stared; then she sped onward to reach my mother swiftly. We could already hear weeping and lamenting voices in the encampment.

Mother was standing on our little rock, with Lysia beside her, saying "Athens is burning" in a dull, slow voice, as though she did not know what the words meant.

"You knew they would," said Phryne softly, taking her hand. But I felt a wild surge of joy, a shocking wicked exultation, and a foolish hope—the old life was gone, and maybe I could live forever in the island summer air, running wild and free like a Spartan. Even as I thought this my mother began to reproach Phryne bitterly: the Spartans had not come to help at Marathon, when my father died. They had not held the pass at Thermopylae to keep the Persians out of Attica. Now Athens was in ashes, and Sparta as always was quite safe. And horrified at my mother's unfair words, and at my own wickedness, I, too, began to cry. Just then a light rain began to fall, so that the bands of weeping citizens on the beaches dispersed, and we four had to go within the tent, and sit so close we had to forgive each other. The rain brought down a smell of burning from the air.

After that there was smoke nearly every day, plumes of gray and white on the view of home. Smoke from farms, and from the groves of olive trees, which take ten years to grow and fruit again. Everyone was miserable, angry and helpless and afraid. I was ashamed to feel happy. But welfare was built into my legs, into my springy step, my agile climbing and running. I couldn't stop it. By day I ran about, or listened to the boys' lessons; at night I slept sweetly, but lightly, waking easily at small sounds.

So I woke when the men came past us. I heard their footsteps lightly grinding the pebbles on the shore. I sat up at once, heart pounding, ears pricked. For ours was the farthest camp of the Athenians—a little way off from the nearest of our neighbors' fires—Phryne had seen to that. Camping too close together breeds sickness, she had said, and so does camping too near the supply of water. The army, the fighting men of so many cities, were farther off still, by the ships. So who came now, in deep darkness, past our tent?

I crept out, crawling low, and moving slowly, and looked out between our rocks. A party of men were moving along the beach, carrying a small boat, and speaking in whispers together. The moon was clouded over, and I could see them only as shadows against the star-gleam on the water. They were wrapped in dark cloaks, I think. But I heard the splash as the little boat went into the water; I heard the oars plashing as it pulled away. I heard a muted voice, raised a little, call, "Farewell! Don't get caught!" I heard departing footfalls along the beach.

What did they mean, "Don't get caught"? I wondered. We were all friends and allies on the island; a boat had only to hug the shore to go safely between one camp and another. But then, going between one camp and another a boat had no need to go at night, those who sent it had no need to whisper. A dreadful fear crept over me, and I began to tremble. What if I had seen—could I have seen—something wicked taking place? I told myself that no Greek could be so evil as to send secretly to those across the water . . . over and over I told myself, but still I scanned the darkness anxiously for any glimpse of the movement of that boat. Then the moon swam out, and I saw the boat plain, far, far out, more than halfway over, the foam from its oars catching the silver light. And then I knew for certain that it was crossing the strait; going home; going in secret to the Persians. Someone was working treachery!

But it's all right, I told myself, hugging my ribs in terror. It's all right; they have been seen. You can tell someone, warn them, foil the plot! *I* can? How can I go anywhere beyond the encampment except with Phryne? Then I must tell Phryne, and take her. But what if it is the Spartans who are betraying us all? What will Phryne do? Will she take our part against her own city? It isn't fair to ask Phryne, said a fierce deep voice inside me. You must do it alone. Do what? Go to the generals. Tell them. Tell who? Oh, the great gods! how do I know who to tell, when any of them may have done it? What if I tell the traitor himself, what then? I should be in great danger, and the last chance would be lost, and the treachery would run its course!

I knew I had to think harder. I drank deeply from the water jar, and sat down, trying wildly to be calm and wise. I would tell only an Athenian; who knows what the men of other cities may be up to? But we have already lost our city and our lands, and having only ourselves left to lose, must needs be steadfast now. But supposing the traitor *is* an Athenian? What do I know about politics? What do I know about men? Well, I do know that my mother thought Kimon worth following, and he was following Themistocles, this once at least. I must tell Themistocles, and him only. And if Mother knows about it she will stop me—she will tell people, and send messages; then the whole camp will know about it before the commanders hear, and anyone in the camp may be among the traitors. I must go alone; now; secretly.

When I knew that, I trembled. I tried to imagine walking through the people, and through the army, right to the generals' tent. I would be stopped. Girls simply did not go alone. Only girls so lost to virtue that they were in search of men . . . and slaves. Slaves! I grabbed the cooking knife, and sitting cross-legged, with bent head, I began to hack off my hair. I was trying to crop it as short as a boy's, or as Lysia's; but with no mirror to see by I overdid it rather. I felt the soft fall of the long tresses against my legs in the dark. My head felt suddenly light; I shook it, and felt the heavy curtain of my hair swing at my ears. Then I took off my fine woven girdle, and put on the simple cord that Lysia wore. I looked up to the stars, asked the gods to protect me, and set off.

The encampment seemed to stretch for miles. I walked on, making my way from one dimly glowing fireside to another, past sleeping forms. I do not remember crossing from the citizens' to the soldiers' camp. But I found myself walking in the gray moonlight by fires surrounded by clumps of spears, planted upright like barren saplings. Once someone called out to me, making me nearly jump out of my skin. I pretended not to understand, and walked on without turning my head. I felt sure it was not really happening, so like a nightmare was it—walking in a strange place with shadowy figures all around me, and some immensely important errand driving me on.

I knew which tent was the generals', for the insignia of all the cities were planted around it on poles. I suppose I had imagined I could just walk up to it, and go in. I walked straight into a little group of guards. Suddenly two spears came down from the right and left of me, and crossed with a click across my path. A voice said, "Where do you think *you're* going?"

"I have to see Themistocles," I said.

"Carrying a letter, are you?" the voice replied. It was so dark I could not see who spoke—the voices came from the shadows under faintly moonlit helmets. "Give it here. I'll see he gets it."

"Not a letter. A message. I have to speak with him."

"You're a funny kind of message boy. Who's this message from?"

I felt sick with fear. I could never talk my way past them. I suddenly ducked under the spears, and ran like Hare toward the tent door.

They caught me from behind, roughly, and lifted me off my feet. I screamed, and fought like a wildcat, drumming vainly with feet and fists.

"Great gods!" said the man who held me, "it's a girl!" And he put me back on my feet, and held me hard by the hair. *"Now,* young whore," he said. "Tell us what you are up to."

I didn't answer him. I opened my mouth as wide as it would go and screamed, "Themistocles!" I got it out twice before a huge hand was thrust across my mouth, gagging me.

But a man came out of the tent, carrying a bright torch, which he held up to us. "Who is calling me?" he asked. He wasn't what I expected; he didn't look like young Kimon. He was short and wide, and heavy, with a coarse, friendly face—as unlike a warrior painted on a vase as he well could be.

"This wench tried to get past us," said the guard.

"Let her speak," said Themistocles.

"Oh, sire, I must speak, and to you only!" I cried, and by now tears were pouring down my face. The guards had not held me gently, and my bruises were aching.

"Come, then," he said, and led me away by the hand to a tent of his own. "Five minutes only can I spare for you," he said to me sternly. But telling him how I had seen the boat cross over the channel, about one hour since, and how I had come straightaway to tell him, did not take so long.

What I said troubled him. He looked long at me, and very intently. Then he said, "Little maid, I must trust you. For it was I who sent the boat. And nobody must know about it."

I let out a wail of dismay, accusing the gods of cruelty who had let me come to the one wrong man, when I had tried so hard to think how not to.

"Hush," he said, smiling at me. "I will explain to you, just a little. You see, we *want* the Persians to attack us here. If they attack us here, very likely we will win, in spite of their great numbers. But they are taking a long time about it. And some of *our* generals would rather fall back, nearer their own cities. So I have played a trick on everybody. It is not for nothing I am called the Fox! I have sent the king a message, saying that we are about to flee, under cover of darkness tomorrow night. If he takes the bait he will come after us, expecting no resistance, and he will find us ready. But this must not be known; there are too many people here for the keeping of secrets, and news may reach the Persians. So you see, the safety of us all and the success of my plan depend on your keeping your tongue till tomorrow. And if you manage that, I will buy you your freedom when our troubles are over."

"Oh, sire," I said, holding my shorn head high. "I am not a slave. I cut my hair off just now, to pass unnoticed on the way to you. But I am a freeborn Athenian, a daughter of one who died at Marathon. And of course I can keep quiet for the sake of my city!"

Then he really smiled at me. "Xerxes didn't know what he was up against, picking on us!" he said. "Be off with you now. It is getting light."

I was in such disgrace when I got back! Phryne had found my dark hair lying on the grass; Lysia had found my girdle in place of hers. And when I returned with bruised arms and shoulders, and a swollen lip, where the guard had held me tight to silence me, and when I would not say where I had been or why, there was uproar. My mother thought first I had been carried off by villains, and was silent from shock. Very soon neighbors had told her I had been seen walking off on my own. Then my mother began to think the worst of me.

At first I said, "I will tell you tomorrow." Then I said, "Whatever I tell you, you will not believe me. How ready you are to think ill of me!"

"Really, girl," said Phryne, "what could you expect people to think?"

"You are disgraced utterly," my mother told me. "You will be fit for nothing but a flute girl, for nobody decent will marry you, with such an episode as this smirching your reputation!"

"*I don't care!*" I cried at last. "At least if I'm a flute girl I can come and go as I please, and see the sun, instead of being shut up all day with a horrible rattling loom, and all that dusty wool!"

Then they would not talk to me at all. But since half the camp knew of my disappearance, and my mother was so distraught, I had only too much reason to fear she would tell all and sundry the explanation, if once she knew it. And so even when Phryne came and took my hand, and said, "Come, pet, tell your old Phryne all about it," I kept silent.

How I would have borne all this if I had not known about the battle, I cannot think. But all the while I *knew* about tomorrow. Tomorrow the Persians would come, they would fall into a trap, they would die! With that thought to comfort me I lived through my terrible day, sitting on a rock by our tent, with a cloak wrapped to cover my shorn head. Little boys came to stare at me, and snigger, but Phryne chased them off.

That night I woke, and rose, and went out into the night to listen. I thought I heard the splashing of oars, the creaking of timber, coming to me faintly over the still water. I grinned to myself, thinking of the Persians tiring themselves out at the oar, waiting for an enemy to come escaping past them, who would not come, but were sleeping quietly, gathering strength for the morning! Oh, just let the morning come!

And when it came, instead of the golden calm of still waters, there were the warships of the Persians, filling the strait, hundreds of them, and crowding onward as far as the eye could see, terrible and splendid, blazing with armed men on the decks. Their raked ranks of oars beat like wings, and churned the sea to frothy white; they cawed to each other with the hoarse voices of brazen trumpets.

Cries of terror and dismay rang from the camp of the people, while I laughed with joy and gladness! It had worked; they had come to their doom; and I was the only one that knew it was a triumph and not a disaster.

Then, even as people began to run, as if to warn unsuspecting generals that the enemy were upon them, we heard another sound—the deep quiet sound of men singing. Hidden behind the promontory our ships were on the move; and hundreds of Greek voices were singing the solemn paean to our gods. Within minutes the line of our ships came into view, moving across the strait to close it to the Persians, and swinging around to meet them head on.

Upon so terrible a sight as that battle I could not look long; my heart had not the strength for it. I watched the first line of the Persians come up to our ships; I heard cries, and trumpets, and the loud rending of splintered hulls. I saw that the Persians were pressing forward too fast, just where the channel narrowed like a funnel, and they were fouling one another's oars, and coming to a helpless standstill just within reach of harm. And I laughed, and was as proud of Themistocles as though he had been brother or father of mine. But I could not look long.

At noon I climbed the height, and looked down at the whole crooked channel choked with ships. I could not discern what was happening, or, from so far off, clearly tell our ships from theirs, but I could see from far off more ships coming up to help them. And I thought we could not possibly win against so many.

Toward evening, when they began to flee away, past us, all broken and disabled, and with our triremes in full pursuit, I looked again. And the water was all curdled and thick with wreckage, and with floating men. A foul detritus of smashed timber and dead men had washed up on the beaches. The dead wore strange armor, with overlapping scales like lizards', and their wounds were washed white by the sea. I crept away, and hid myself in our tent, and took no part in the joy and dancing, and celebrating among the people.

The next day brought truer joy to me. The Persians did not come back; we had won a sufficient victory. But Nikias came, stooping through the tent door to say to my mother, "So here you all are! I thought I should never find you!" He took me in one hard arm, and my mother in another, and showed her the gash in his hand that some Persian had yesterday paid for with his life.

"Oh, Nikias!" said my mother in a while. "So terrible a thing has happened. Aster has ruined herself."

"Why, whatever have you done, pet?" said Nikias, turning to me.

"Would you believe your sister could have cropped her hair, and gone off among the army?" said my mother bitterly. "Who will marry her after such a thing?"

And suddenly, framed in the tent door, there was Themistocles, all in bronze. "So the little maid came safe home again, I see," he said, "and has kept her promise of silence well and truly. Madam, I think indeed that one of my young men would be proud to take as wife so brave and spirited a girl as yours, whatever clacking tongues may have said against her."

"Oh, Themistocles!" I cried. "I don't want to be married, to be kept indoors all day, and never breathe the open air!"

He laughed. "Why, then, you need, I should think, a man with a Spartan mother, and liberal views, and an estate in the country somewhere healthy and secluded," he said. There were several young men with him, and he was looking now particularly at one of them, and that one was smiling at me.

"Little maid, shorn hair soon grows again," he said to me. And to my mother, "I am Androcles, son of Leontes, madam. And when we are home again my family will approach your son, and ask for his sister for me."

I would have looked at him, but the bright light off his armor dazzled me. I smiled, but I looked down at my two hands folded meekly in my lap.

K. M. Peyton, "A Man and a Boy"

The Thames, with London on its banks one of the world's busiest rivers, was once marked by the distinctive reddish sails of the barges used to haul freight around the east coast of England. As power vessels took their places, some of the Thames sailing barges were simply left to rot. So it is with the *Emma Louise,* the barge that has always been part of the landscape outside Martin's bedroom window, lifting regularly with the tide and settling once more into the mud of a Kentish estuary. Martin and his friends are warned against playing on the barge by a blustery shoe-store owner—called Sailorman, with a wink, by the old boys in the pub—who begins repairing the craft and boasting of the voyages he'll take. Drawn back to the barge, Martin begins to realize that the *Emma Louise* will never sail with such a man at its helm. Martin seems to reflect the boat's own urge to set sail once again, as it does for a final time with its traditional crew—just a man and a boy.

A Man and a Boy
by K. M. Peyton

IT WAS FRIDAY night, the night the Sailorman came down from London in his E-type Jaguar. Martin hopped about on the muddy shore, waiting for the little Friday night pantomime, to see the Sailorman go aboard his barge.

The barge had lain on the shore of the Kentish estuary ever since Martin could remember. He was ten, and from his bedroom window he could see the barge; had always seen the barge, ever since he was little. She was called *Emma Louise*. She was an old Thames sailing-barge which had once carried freight around the East coast shores, crewed by just a skipper and a mate. "A man and a boy," as the locals put it, or even "a man and his wife." Eighty feet long, driven by five thousand square feet of tanned flax sail, she had carried corn, coal, fertilizer, stone, and pitch until her owners had decided that motor coasters were the thing. One by one the sailing barges were laid up, or cut down into lighters, or motorized, or sold as houseboats. *Emma Louise* had been left to rot. She *had* rotted. Martin had played in her gaunt mud-carpeted hold, big as a ballroom, ever since he could remember. With the other village boys he had made fires in her cabin stove, cooked sausages, pulled out her paneling to burn, swung on her shrouds, and climbed her mast. Until, one weekend, the Sailorman had arrived on the scene.

"If I catch you little beggars anywhere near my barge I'll tan the daylights out of you!" he had roared.

And he had so obviously meant it that the gang had scattered, and thereafter troubled *Emma Louise* no more. Except Martin. He never went aboard again, but he used to play on the shore, watching. He watched the Sailorman every weekend and learned all about what the Sailorman was going to do, through overhearing bits of conversation. He knew that the Sailorman owned a chain of shoe shops and was very rich. He was going to turn *Emma Louise* into "a floating palace." He knew all there was to know about sailing. He boasted about how he was going to sail *Emma Louise* around the estuary. . . . "Handy as a dinghy when you know how to handle them. Lovely craft. I could take her through the moorings on a dead beat and not turn a hair. It's just knowing the ropes, literally." For years the Sailorman had been going to sail *Emma Louise* "like a dinghy." He had had a new suit of sails made. They were bent on, dark brown and virgin on the scraped and varnished spars. *Emma Louise* was refitted like a queen and the Sailorman kept talking about when he would take her to the Solent . . . "winter in the Med" . . . "the Bay of Biscay would be nothing to her. . . ." But the weed hung green on her mooring warps and the tide lifted her twice a day, and then she lay down on the mud again, where she had lain for all of Martin's ten years, and she never moved out.

"Why does he talk about it so?" Martin wondered.

It was the old boys in the village who had called him the Sailorman. "Right old Sailorman," they said, and winked. The Sailorman stood them all drinks in the pub on Saturday night and told them how easy she was on the wheel. He wore an old navy-blue jersey and sailcloth trousers tucked into gum boots; he smoked a pipe and was more of a sailorman than the sailormen themselves.

"Man and boy used to sail these ships . . . easiest ships in the world to sail. . . ."

"No! Really?" said the old boys, winking. "Mine'll be a bitter, thank you very much, sir."

Martin waited and waited for *Emma Louise* to sail. He longed to see her lovely expensive sails uncurl from their brails and stretch to a Kentish breeze over the estuary. But the Sailorman went on talking, and unloading new gear out of his Jaguar every Friday night, and he could spend all the weekend polishing a brass skylight and examining the new rigging that had been fitted during the week by the shipwright on the hard, and the tide would lift *Emma Louise* four times before he drove back to London, and not once would he take advantage of it and sail out.

"Blooming shame," said the old boy on the beach.

Martin eased a worn sandal out of the mud and looked at the old boy curiously. He had only lately come to live in the village. His name was Bob. He had been on a ship all his life and now he had retired he spent a lot of time on the beach looking for things the tide turned up and looking at the coasters going up to Rochester. Martin knew him well by sight. But today he looked at *Emma Louise* and said to Martin, "Blooming shame."

"What is?" said Martin.

"The old girl here. All that money wasted—new sails! It's a new hull the old girl wants. She's falling to pieces. Built eighteen eighty-five, she was, you know that? At Maldon. One of Howard's." He shook his head. "That man who bought her, he's crazy."

"The Bay of Biscay, he says," said Martin.

Bob laughed. He laughed until he started to cough,

and his faded eyes watered painfully. "Bay of Biscay? Oh, dear."

Martin grinned. "Don't you think——?"

"Dear me. No. She'll never move again. I was skipper of her once, you know. Just after the First World War."

Martin's eyebrows shot up. *Really?*

"That's right. Had a boy for a mate, bit like you. All the grown men were killed in the war."

"You *sailed* her?"

"Yes. Five years I was her skipper."

"Oh!" Martin looked at Bob as if he were a shining angel.

"That man," said Bob, "he's spent a fortune on her. Don't know what to do with his money, same as he wouldn't know what to do with the boat if he cast the mooring warps off her."

"You would, though."

"Oh, aye. You don't forget."

"I'd love to see her sail," Martin said.

"Aye, they're lovely things. You don't see 'em now."

"It's true it takes just a man and a boy?"

"Aye. That's the beauty of 'em. Carry a hundred and eighty ton, and just needs the two of you."

"You and me."

Bob laughed. "Aye. You and me."

All the summer the Sailorman worked on *Emma Louise.* Martin had his eleventh birthday, and *Emma Louise* was painted by a man from Rochester. Her name was done in gold and her scrollwork in pale and dark blue, her seamy sides black with a big yellow line around. She lifted on the tide, and settled, and lifted, all through the winter, and the unused sails lay brailed snugly on the sprit. Martin used to meet Bob sometimes on the beach, trying not to remember that his mother called Bob a scruffy old beachcomber. He was with Bob one Sunday evening when the Sailorman left to go back to London, and they watched him as he came down the ladder with his smart kit-bag over his shoulder. He had a woman with him, a very elegant woman with high heels, and Martin knew that she was not the Bay of Biscay type.

"Oh, Bob!" he said.

It was a lovely evening. The tide was ebbing and a half-moon was hanging in the sky over the river. Martin didn't want to go home. He wanted to sail *Emma Louise*.

"Bob, we could," he said, "if we wanted to. She'll be afloat for half an hour yet. We could sail her out and back on the flood and have her all moored up again before morning."

Bob looked at him, sideways. From up on the quay a car door slammed, and the noise of the Jaguar's engine shivered through the dusk.

"You know what?" Bob said conversationally. "What you say is not so daft as it sounds. We couldn't get into trouble for it. Tell you for why: there ain't no law of trespass on a boat. If we don't hurt her, he couldn't come it. We could just laugh."

"Oh, Bob, let's," Martin said. He had never realized before how easy it would be. On a night like this with a faint breeze from the west, a moon to steer by, and smell of spring stirring the impulses. It seemed a terribly easy thing to do.

"I wouldn't mind standing at the wheel of a barge again," Bob said.

"Please," said Martin.

Bob stirred the mud with his toe, pulling on his fag end so that a small glow went up from the promontory of his nose like the loom of a miniature lighthouse. Martin fixed his eyes on it and prayed.

"Nothing to lose," Bob said.

He threw the fag end down suddenly and Martin heard it hiss in the mud. The next moment he was scuffling up the beach to where a flotsam of small boats lay pulled up above the high-water mark.

"Get my little fishing boat," he muttered. "And a sculling oar——"

Martin couldn't believe it. It was almost as if he were standing there, watching an old man and a scruffy boy with red hair shoving the rowing boat down into the water. It went afloat with a quick-silvering of phosphorescence round the bows. The man and the boy got in and the old man fixed a sculling blade in the stern and sculled out to the barge. "But it *is* me," Martin said to himself, staring.

They went aboard silently, and made the rowing boat fast to the stern of the barge. It all happened very quickly. Bob walked round the decks and cast off the mooring warps one by one, and the ebb and the breeze took *Emma Louise* off from the beach. One moment the beach was there, their footsteps tracking black across its sheen; the next there was water all around them and the few lights above the sea wall were far away. Martin found that he was standing in front of the wheel. From somewhere in the darkness in front of him Bob's voice floated back, "Helm down to port," and Martin was aware of a topsail breaking into flower way above his head with a lovely waft of tar-smelling new rope. Martin tried to remember whether port was left or right. He put his hands on the wheel and felt it move of its own volition. Port is left, he thought, and moved the wheel anticlockwise, clutching its big spokes with sweaty fingers. He could hear a great rushing of water all around him, and the thumping of his own heart right up in his throat, like an engine. What have we done? he thought, still turning the wheel. What have we done?

"Steady on, lad. You'll have us back ashore."

Bob was at his shoulder, pushing the wheel back the other way. "There. As she goes. Steer for that flashing light. That marks the channel."

"Is it all right, then?"

"Of course it's all right. What do you think?" Bob chuckled.

The topsail was drawing, black against the luminous pale-green tracery of the stars. Soon mainsail and staysail were drawing, too, the weather leeboard was dropped down, and the old barge was slipping along like a yacht.

Bob came and stood by Martin at the wheel, and Martin said, "Here. You're the skipper," and handed over. He was scared and incredulous, feeling the deck alive and moving under his feet. The dark sails, exulting in their baptism, seemed to fill the whole sky.

"Very naughty," Bob was saying, chuckling at the words. "We're very naughty, eh, Martin?"

"Oh, yes."

But now Bob was in charge Martin felt the excitement creeping up, washing out his scariness. After all, they weren't stealing her. And she was beautiful. She was all movement, sheets creaking, water hissing off the rudder, creaming with a white bow-wave off the dipping lee-board. The flashing channel light was coming at them steadily and beyond again Martin could see the next one, and another to make a pair. Two more shakes of the river and they would be out in the estuary among the ships coming down from London. Martin gave a little shiver. And this was *Emma Louise,* this hurrying, rustling, creaking, hustling ship . . . *Emma Louise* who had lain for so long in the mud that she had almost dug out her own grave. Whatever happened, he was glad they had done it.

"Where shall we go?" Bob said. "Bay of Biscay?" He started to laugh, until the wheezing cough stopped him. "Leak like a sieve, she would, if she had to beat into a sea. Open up like a bit of knitting."

"This is her weather," Martin said. "Gentle."

"Aye. Gentle for an old lady."

"I bet she's enjoying herself," Martin said.

"Aye, she told me so. All done out in her new skirts. Thinks she's a gel again."

Martin could tell that Bob was enjoying himself too. As the barge came up to the flashing buoy, he eased the wheel, and pulled hard on his fag end, and the buoy went past them with a red wink, very close, so that the springing of its flash gave Martin a fright, although he had been watching for it. Martin thought the old barge was smelling the sea. With the ebb under her, she reached out through the Kentish marshes, steering by the lit buoys that flicked and flashed like will-o'-the-wisps, until Martin could smell the sweet, sickly smell of the oil refineries on the Isle of Grain. Beyond was the mouth of the River Thames, he knew, and the North Foreland and the North Sea, the highway of the big ships. He felt his stomach give a nervous quiver.

"Where are we going?"

"Just put our nose out, eh?" Bob said. "Then home soon as the tide turns."

"Did you ever come this way in her, before?"

"Oh, aye. Many a time. Up to Beckton or Wapping, or up-Swin. She knows the way all right."

The moon was breaking out at the masthead, flooding the black creeks and marshes on their starboard hand with a cold, sharp light. A solitary duck put up a ripple of silver, and a wader called forlornly, the lonely cry carrying over the eager progress of the barge. But ahead of them the refineries were glowing and stinking, and the tankers lay in lines along the jetties.

"We'll go out to the Noll, and come back as soon as the tide starts making. It runs very strong off Garrison Point. She'll not make in again till it turns," Bob said.

The dark marshes gave way to the lights of Queenborough and Sheerness, and soon the Isle of Grain shore had curved away to the north and Martin found himself looking clean across the broad silver breast of the Thames to the lights of Southend on the Essex shore. A galaxy of flashing buoys stuttered in their path, and a big liner, lit like a Christmas tree, was going down with the heavy thump of her screws throbbing on the breeze. Martin had his detached feeling again, watching himself watching the liner and, with a shaft of piercing guilt, wondering whatever had possessed them to sail *Emma Louise*. But the night could not be soured by fear. The small detached Martin knew that this night was quite inviolate; whatever happened, the magic could not be erased. He looked at every detail in every direction, hungry not to miss a thing, not the realist reek of the oil nor the prettiest twinkle of a reflected star. They would never do it again, he thought, not himself, nor Bob. Nor *Emma Louise*.

A small coaster came up behind them, and Bob changed course slightly to give it more room.

"I thought steam gave way to sail," Martin said.

"Once upon a time," said Bob. "But now all the sail is pleasure, just about, and pleasure gives way to work. He's working. We're—we're cruising." The last phrase seemed to give him great amusement. He repeated it: "We're cruising," and laughed till the cough choked him.

Martin watched the little men on the bridge of the coaster, and a man silhouetted in a bright doorway. The man waved at them and the coaster went past with the rough thumping of her diesel and a wash that *Emma Louise* pushed scornfully aside. Bob started to put the wheel over.

"The tide's on the turn. We'd best be getting back before they notice the old girl's missing."

The barge went about and Bob went forward to make fast the staysail sheet, and Martin took the wheel. It was a soldier's wind for their outing, light and from the north, fair for coming and fair for going, Martin thought. Bob made no move to take over the wheel again, and Martin sailed *Emma Louise* home. He felt he had waited all his eleven years for this night, and felt no more fear, not even any more amazement, just a glowing satisfaction. It was as if *Emma Louise* were coming up through the soles of his feet and sailing herself.

The lights were out over the sea wall and nothing moved on the home beach.

"We'll put her aground and warp her back into her berth," Bob said. "The tide'll do the work, while it's making."

He went forward to the mast, and presently the big mainsail started to take up like a stage curtain. Bob was turning the winch handle and the sail was returning to its brailed-up position on the mast, its great mass extinguished by one old man still drawing on his fag end. Martin felt the stars bursting out over his head, as if a cloud had dissolved.

"Hard over now. Put her just up-tide of her berth."

Bob was dropping the staysail. Under topsail alone *Emma Louise* slipped into the shore until the mud caught her and she slewed round, facing up into the tide. Bob dropped the topsail, then took a warp from her bows ashore in the dinghy and made it fast to one of the big rusted anchors buried in the beach. Everything was quiet now. Bob came back aboard and rolled another thin cigarette.

"We wait a bit now, then free off the warp when the tide's made a bit more, and she'll slip back in her old berth, no trouble."

"It's so easy," Martin said wonderingly.

"It's easy weather," Bob said. "It's not always easy. Not just for a man and a boy, sometimes, when you're working to windward in a big blow, trying to make harbor perhaps, and the tide about to turn on you, and the barge heavy-loaded and making water like a broken bucket. . . ."

But it was easy tonight. *Emma Louise* was moored up to her four warps; sails, sheets, and halyards left as they had been found, footmarks swabbed off the deck. Bob and Martin went ashore in Bob's dinghy and pulled it up the beach. The moon sailed gloriously over the river and the tide kept on creeping up, erasing footmarks and dinghy trails. They went up over the sea wall, and turned round to look back at the barge.

Martin touched Bob's arm suddenly.

"Look! She's the wrong way round! Her bows are pointing down the river. They were pointing up before."

"Aye," said Bob.

"I never thought about it," Martin said anxiously. "Didn't you notice?"

"Aye, I did," said Bob.

"The Sailorman'll see."

"The fairies done it," Bob said.

Shirley Jackson, "Charles"

The narrator of this story notices a certain swagger as her son rounds the corner on the way to his first day in kindergarten. More disturbing, though, is what her son Laurie brings home with him, including questionable grammar, a collection of disrespectful remarks, and fascinating tales of the class terror, Charles. Unfortunately, we never witness Charles's stunts because it is Laurie's mother telling the story, and we must wait with her for his latest eager report at the lunch table: hitting the teacher, throwing chalk, kicking a gym instructor, bouncing a seesaw on a girl's head, and suggesting foul language for use by other students (when Charles was not using it himself). But it seems that being there, at least in this case, would spoil the fun.

"Charles"

by Shirley Jackson

THE DAY MY SON Laurie started kindergarten he renounced corduroy overalls with bibs and began wearing blue jeans with a belt; I watched him go off the first morning with the older girl next door, seeing clearly that an era of my life was ended, my sweet-voiced nursery-school tot replaced by a long-trousered, swaggering character who forgot to stop at the corner and wave good-bye to me.

He came home the same way, the front door slamming open, his cap on the floor, and the voice suddenly become raucous shouting: "Isn't anybody *here?*"

At lunch he spoke insolently to his father, spilled his baby sister's milk, and remarked that his teacher said we were not to take the name of the Lord in vain.

"How *was* school today?" I asked, elaborately casual.

"All right," he said.

"Did you learn anything?" his father asked.

Laurie regarded his father coldly. "I didn't learn nothing," he said.

"Anything," I said. "Didn't learn anything."

"The teacher spanked a boy, though," Laurie said, addressing his bread and butter. "For being fresh," he added, with his mouth full.

"What did he do?" I asked. "Who was it?"

Laurie thought. "It was Charles," he said. "He was fresh. The teacher spanked him and made him stand in a corner. He was awfully fresh."

"What did he do?" I asked again, but Laurie slid off

his chair, took a cookie, and left, while his father was still saying, "See here, young man."

The next day Laurie remarked at lunch, as soon as he sat down, "Well, Charles was bad again today." He grinned enormously and said, "Today Charles hit the teacher."

"Good heavens," I said, mindful of the Lord's name, "I suppose he got spanked again?"

"He sure did," Laurie said. "Look up," he said to his father.

"What?" his father said, looking up.

"Look down," Laurie said. "Look at my thumb. Gee, you're dumb." He began to laugh insanely.

"Why did Charles hit the teacher?" I asked quickly.

"Because she tried to make him color with red crayons," Laurie said. "Charles wanted to color with green crayons so he hit the teacher and she spanked him and said nobody play with Charles but everybody did."

The third day—it was Wednesday of the first week—Charles bounced a seesaw onto the head of a little girl and made her bleed, and the teacher made him stay inside all during recess. Thursday Charles had to stand in a corner during story time because he kept pounding his feet on the floor. Friday Charles was deprived of blackboard privileges because he threw chalk.

On Saturday I remarked to my husband, "Do you think kindergarten is too unsettling for Laurie? All this toughness, and bad grammar, and this Charles boy sounds like such a bad influence."

"It'll be all right," my husband said reassuringly. "Bound to be people like Charles in the world. Might as well meet them now as later."

On Monday Laurie came home late, full of news.

"Charles," he shouted as he came up the hill; I was waiting anxiously on the front steps. "Charles," Laurie yelled all the way up the hill, "Charles was bad again."

"Come right in," I said, as soon as he came close enough. "Lunch is waiting."

"You know what Charles did?" he demanded, following me through the door. "Charles yelled so in school they sent a boy in from first grade to tell the teacher she had to make Charles keep quiet, and so Charles had to stay after school. And so all the children stayed to watch him."

"What did he do?" I asked.

"He just sat there," Laurie said, climbing into his chair at the table. "Hi, Pop, y'old dust mop."

"Charles had to stay after school today," I told my husband. "Everyone stayed with him."

"What does this Charles look like?" my husband asked Laurie. "What's his other name?"

"He's bigger than me," Laurie said. "And he doesn't have any rubbers and he doesn't ever wear a jacket."

Monday night was the first Parent-Teachers meeting, and only the fact that the baby had a cold kept me from going; I wanted passionately to meet Charles's mother. On Tuesday Laurie remarked suddenly, "Our teacher had a friend come to see her in school today."

"Charles's mother?" my husband and I asked simultaneously.

"Naaah," Laurie said scornfully. "It was a man who came and made us do exercises, we had to touch our toes. Look." He climbed down from his chair and squatted down and touched his toes. "Like this," he said. He got solemnly back into his chair and said, picking up his fork, "Charles didn't even *do* exercises."

"That's fine," I said heartily. "Didn't Charles want to do exercises?"

"Naaah," Laurie said. "Charles was so fresh to the teacher's friend he wasn't *let* do exercises."

"Fresh again?" I said.

"He kicked the teacher's friend," Laurie said. "The teacher's friend told Charles to touch his toes like I just did and Charles kicked him."

"What are they going to do about Charles, do you suppose?" Laurie's father asked him.

Laurie shrugged elaborately. "Throw him out of school, I guess," he said.

Wednesday and Thursday were routine; Charles yelled during story hour and hit a boy in the stomach and made him cry. On Friday Charles stayed after school again and so did all the other children.

With the third week of kindergarten Charles was an institution in our family; the baby was being a Charles when she cried all afternoon; Laurie did a Charles when he filled his wagon full of mud and pulled it through the kitchen; even my husband, when he caught his elbow in the telephone cord and pulled telephone, ashtray, and a bowl of flowers off the table, said, after the first minute, "Looks like Charles."

During the third and fourth weeks it looked like a reformation in Charles; Laurie reported grimly at lunch on Thursday of the third week, "Charles was so good today the teacher gave him an apple."

"What?" I said, and my husband added warily, "You mean Charles?"

"Charles," Laurie said. "He gave the crayons around and he picked up the books afterward and the teacher said he was her helper."

"What happened?" I asked incredulously.

"He was her helper, that's all," Laurie said, and shrugged.

"Can this be true, about Charles?" I asked my husband that night. "Can something like this happen?"

"Wait and see," my husband said cynically. "When you've got a Charles to deal with, this may mean he's only plotting."

He seemed to be wrong. For over a week Charles was the teacher's helper; each day he handed things out and he picked things up; no one had to stay after school.

"The PTA meeting's next week again," I told my husband one evening. "I'm going to find Charles's mother there."

"Ask her what happened to Charles," my husband said. "I'd like to know."

"I'd like to know myself," I said.

On Friday of that week things were back to normal. "You know what Charles did today?" Laurie demanded at the lunch table, in a voice slightly awed. "He told a little girl to say a word and she said it and the teacher washed her mouth out with soap and Charles laughed."

"What word?" his father asked unwisely, and Laurie said, "I'll have to whisper it to you, it's so bad." He got down off his chair and went around to his father. His father bent his head down and Laurie whispered joyfully. His father's eyes widened.

"Did Charles tell the little girl to say *that?*" he asked respectfully.

"She said it *twice,*" Laurie said. "Charles told her to say it *twice.*"

"What happened to Charles?" my husband asked.

"Nothing," Laurie said. "He was passing out the crayons."

Monday morning Charles abandoned the little girl and said the evil word himself three or four times, getting his mouth washed out with soap each time. He also threw chalk.

My husband came to the door with me that evening as I set out for the PTA meeting. "Invite her over for a cup of tea after the meeting," he said. "I want to get a look at her."

"If only she's there," I said prayerfully.

"She'll be there," my husband said. "I don't see how they could hold a PTA meeting without Charles's mother."

At the meeting I sat restlessly, scanning each comfortable matronly face, trying to determine which one hid the secret of Charles. None of them looked to me haggard enough. No one stood up in the meeting and apologized for the way her son had been acting. No one mentioned Charles.

After the meeting I identified and sought out Laurie's kindergarten teacher. She had a plate with a cup of tea and a piece of chocolate cake; I had a plate with a cup of tea and a piece of marshmallow cake. We maneuvered up to one another cautiously, and smiled.

"I've been so anxious to meet you," I said. "I'm Laurie's mother."

"We're all so interested in Laurie," she said.

"Well, he certainly likes kindergarten," I said. "He talks about it all the time."

"We had a little trouble adjusting, the first week or so," she said primly, "but now he's a fine little helper. With occasional lapses, of course."

"Laurie usually adjusts very quickly," I said. "I suppose this time it's Charles's influence."

"Charles?"

"Yes," I said, laughing, "you must have your hands full in that kindergarten, with Charles."

"Charles?" she said. "We don't have any Charles in the kindergarten."

Kevin Crossley-Holland,
"The Horseman"

The day is gray and tending toward rain. Outside a rude hut two children await the return of their father, who has joined an English force against a band of plundering Danes. The sea rovers have long plagued the Anglo-Saxons, Germanic tribes who left their crowded homelands and established themselves in Britain beginning in the fifth century.

It is 991. Encamped on an island in the River Blackwater near Maldon in Essex, and unable to cross the causeway defended by the English, the Danes convince the proud leader Byrhtnoth to let them come ashore in the interests of a fair fight.[1] The famous Anglo-Saxon poem *The Battle of Maldon* speaks less of a fair fight than of a bloody rout of the English. That poem also offers a clear statement of the warrior's code—that he shall fight for his lord, and if his lord is killed, avenge his death or die along with him.[2] Cowardice and flight brand a man.

The code is well known even to the young daughter of a lowly farmer who has gone to Maldon to fight with his lord. As Gode keeps watch over the bleak landscape for her father Dunnere's return, it is a stranger, a single horseman, who thunders into their yard bearing unsettling news.

---

[1] J.R.R. Tolkien, *Tree and Leaf; Smith of Wootton Major; The Homecoming of Beorhtnoth, Beorhthelm's Son* (London: Unwin Books, 1975), pp. 149–50.
[2] Bruce Mitchell, ed., and Kevin Crossley-Holland, trans., *The Battle of Maldon, and Other Old English Poems* (London: Macmillan and Company, Limited; New York: St. Martin's Press, Inc. 1967), p. 13.

The Horseman
by Kevin Crossley-Holland

Then Dunnere spoke and shook his spear;
a lowly churl, he cried out loud
and asked every man to avenge Byrhtnoth's death:
"Whoever intends to avenge our prince
must not flinch, nor care for his own life."

"WHO ARE YOU?" demanded the girl Gode.

She had seen him a long way off. Her eagle eye, open for her absent father, singled him out against the dark backdrop of the distant wood. She watched him turn off the sandy road to Colchester and gallop across the acres of scrub, a lonesome figure in a desolate scape.

As soon as she was certain that the rider had left the highway on purpose, and realized he was heading directly for their farm, she called out "Edgar." Her voice was a bell, appealing. And quickly enough her brother, four years old, less than half her age, trotted out of the hut and into the yard, grinning like a little devil. "Demon!" he yelled, "dee-mon!", hoping to provoke her into a small fight.

"Look!" said Gode, pointing, anxious.

And Edgar looked, but in the wrong direction.

Then she took her brother's grubby hand and, stepping back instinctively, they stood together at the entrance to the hut, waiting for the horseman to arrive.

For a moment he seemed to dip out of sight. After that, there was thunder as he spurred his horse up the incline, and into the yard itself. Hens dispersed, squawking.

The rider reined in his great sweating bay; it pawed the ground, and its hooves kicked up little puffs of dust. A helmet hung at the man's side, and he held a spear of ashwood in one hand. He was wearing a mail coat that musically clinked and chinked and gleamed under the gray sky.

"Who are you?" Gode demanded again. But this time her voice quavered.

The man ignored her question. Gasping for breath, he ran a hand through his tangled fair hair. Then he looked over his right shoulder, and for a full minute scanned the lonely plain; apparently satisfied, he glanced about him. "Is there anyone in there?" he asked, staring right through them.

Gode gripped Edgar's hand more fiercely.

"Is there anyone in there?" the warrior rasped. "Where's your father?"

"Are you . . ." Gode began uncertainly.

"I'm as English as you are," said the warrior.

"My father's with Byrhtnoth. He's gone to fight the Danes at Maldon."

The horseman said nothing; there was an uneasy silence. "And your mother?" he asked at length.

Gode dropped her head. "She's dead," she said in a steady expressionless voice. And it was as if with that question the horseman had driven his spear point to her heart. "Dead," she said again, and fiercely, "The Danes killed her."

Then the horseman dismounted.

Gode and Edgar drew back. "I'm not afraid," said Gode.

"You've nothing to be afraid of," said the warrior, and

he put his helmet and spear on the ground as if to prove it.

"What do you want?" asked Gode, confused. "Who are you?"

"Godric," said the man, "and what I want is food. Can you give me that?" He smiled at them encouragingly. "Food, and some bandage for a hurt."

"Where have you come from?" Gode asked him.

"London," said Godric, "with a message from the king, from Ethelred himself to the people of Bradwell and Dengie." And guessing her next question, he went on: "Yes, I came by Maldon. No men were fighting there. No Saxons, no Danes." He shrugged his shoulders.

"But didn't—" began Gode.

Godric interrupted her. "Otherwise, how would I be here? I'd be with them, fighting with your father and with Byrhtnoth at Maldon."

Gode felt troubled in her heart and in her mind. It showed in her eyes. "How can it be?" she said. "My father told me . . . I don't understand. He said the whole fyrd was to gather at Maldon."

Godric shrugged his shoulders again. "I've told you," he said.

"Haven't you heard," Gode insisted, "that Olaf Tryggvason himself leads a great force of Vikings?"

Godric eyed her. "I've told you," he repeated, "I know nothing of it."

"Last week they ravaged Ipswich. Now they're at Maldon"—and Gode pointed accusingly at the distant wood—"camped on an island in the River Blackwater."

"They must have moved on," said Godric. "Those sea-farers are as slippery as eels."

Gode frowned fiercely and shook her head.

"Food," said Godric, "and some bandage for a hurt."

"Come, then," said Gode curtly, and she turned and disappeared into the hut.

All this time Edgar had stood silent. Now, sensing his chance, he said unexpectedly, "Can I have your spear?"

"You can look at it," said Godric, good-naturedly. He handed it to Edgar, who turned the slender stem of ash in his hands, entranced. "I'll throw it," he said, raising it above his shoulder with some difficulty, daring Godric to stop him.

"Come!" called Gode sharply, addressing herself more to Edgar than to their guest.

The seasons of the day made little difference to the inside of the hut. It was a gloomy den, a single room with a hearth at its center; there was smoke but no fire. Pungent animal-skins were stretched over the soil; there was a table, roughly joined, standing in one corner.

"Sit down," said Gode.

And Godric and Edgar sat down. They faced each other across the hearth.

Gode tossed back her pale hair, more composed now, feeling that events were under control; composed, and perhaps even glad to have something to do, glad to escape from herself. For all that endless, empty day, she had been prey to her own teeming fears for her father Dunnere. She looked questioningly at Godric. "Your hurt?" she said.

"Dunnere's doing fighting," Edgar announced proudly.

Godric nodded at Edgar, and he sighed. "Yes," he said. "I know." Then, turning to Gode, he said "It's here." And putting one hand over the other, he pressed his left thigh. "The horse threw me, and my spear's point gashed me when I fell."

Edgar looked interested. "Poorly," he said.

Gode dropped on one knee beside Godric. She saw how his clothing was stained dark with blood, how the cloth had ripped, then stuck to his torn skin. "It's bad," she said. And she was amazed she had not noticed it before.

"It could be worse," said Godric.

"I'll get some water from the well," Gode said.

"No," said Godric sharply.

Edgar's eyes opened very wide. He frowned at the tone of Godric's voice, and edged backwards.

"Is it far?" asked Godric. "I can't wait long."

"It's only across the yard," said Gode. "Edgar will talk with you."

But Edgar would do nothing of the kind. "Wait!" he called unnecessarily, and scrambled to his feet.

Then Gode picked up an earthenware pot and, with Edgar tripping over her heels, walked out of the hut.

Godric looked about him, at the worn sheepskins on the floor, the pans by the hearth; he stared at the gleaming wind-eyes, and at the larger smoke-hole in the roof. Then he leaned back, pillowing his head on the palms of his hands, and closed his eyes.

The two children hurried across the yard to the well. While Gode turned the handle, paying out the rope, Edgar lay on his stomach and leaned over the edge; he peered into the darkness, and pitched little pebbles into the water.

Gode winched the bucket to the surface again; it swung on its long rope, banging against the sides of the well. The sounds it made echoed, and reechoed.

Then, holding the pitcher under one arm, Gode slopped some of the icy water into it. "All right," she said to Edgar.

But Edgar was already making his way, not to the hut, but to what interested him altogether more: Godric's shield and spear.

"Leave them alone," said Gode without any conviction at all. For she, too, was drawn by the weapons, lying there in the dust. She had never seen such glorious wargear: tempered iron, inlaid with garnets and gold, wrought by master smiths. Half drawn, half meaning to restrain Edgar, she stepped forward, and knelt by the weapons.

Then Gode saw it; sharply she drew in her breath. She felt hot and cold, a tingling at the nape of her neck. "Blood," she said disbelievingly, as if her eyes deceived her. They did not. The shield and spear-tip were spattered with blood, blood still red, recently clotted.

"Poorly," declared Edgar.

Gode pushed him away. "Why?" she said. "Why blood?" And her own blood raced within her; her heart thumped so hard that it hurt.

She stood up, pouting as she thought; she wondered what it could mean, what it could possibly mean. A suspicion . . . she dismissed it. Once more Gode felt afraid. And she wished very much that her father, Dunnere, on this day of all days, was not so far from home.

Then she walked across to the great bay, who looked at her with some interest. Her mind was confused; she leaned her head against its comforting warm flank. Her mind was confused: the blood, her father, his danger, her father, the blood, their danger.

Edgar knew something was wrong; he trailed behind Gode and presently tugged at her sleeve.

Suddenly the horse tossed its head and neighed. Gode started, and dismissed her thoughts. She smiled gravely at her brother, mindful of her responsibility for him.

"Look!" said Edgar, pointing with a stubby forefinger. "That's a saggle."

"What?" said Gode.

"Saggle."

"Saddle," Gode corrected him. And even as she said it, she saw the eagle on it inlaid in gold: Byrhtnoth's eagle sign, the emblem of the prince, leader of the East Saxons. And Gode knew at once that this must be, could only be, Byrhtnoth's, Byrhtnoth's bay; and she knew too that Godric must have fought and fled from Maldon that day.

A quiet rain began to fall then, a small mournful rain out of the iron sky.

Gode trembled with fear and fury. She trembled for her father, her father fighting against the sea wolves; and she seethed with anger at Godric's treachery, his calm, his pack of lies. Now she understood why he had not given her his name at first; now she understood why he wanted food; why he had looked nervous when she said she was going for water.

Then, with shaking hands, Gode unfastened the girth and, reaching up, slipped the saddle from the great bay's back. She carried it into the hut. Edgar reeled after her, anxious and clutching the pitcher.

Godric sat up.

And Gode hurled the saddle at his feet.

She looked at him; and for a long moment he looked back at her, then he turned his head away.

"Godric," cried Gode. And then again, less fiercely, no

less passionately, "Godric. Godric. You will live to hate your name as other men will hate it." She hardly knew what to say, there were so many things to say.

"It wasn't a fight," said Godric defensively. "It was a butchery. Byrhtnoth in his pride let the Danes cross the causeway from their island encampment; the Vikings waded across the shallow water. They outnumbered us. Five to one, six to one, they outnumbered us."

Gode looked at him with contempt.

"They shattered the shield wall; those with horses were thrown. I saw Wulfmaer, Byrhtnoth's sister's son, slashed by the sword; corpses floated in the river; the water ran red." Godric closed his eyes. "And Byrhtnoth himself was killed, his neck was slit open. He cried to the Lord, then the heathens hewed him down. Girl, you do not know—"

"I know," interrupted Gode angrily, "that you've stolen your lord's own horse. I know about the oaths of loyalty." She gripped Edgar's hand and, small as he was, or perhaps because he was so small, he gave her greater strength. "My father has told me, told me the duty of every thane and churl. I know you must fight when your lord is slain. You must avenge your lord, or else lie dead beside him."

Then Gode burst into a storm of tears; her whole body shook as the full force of what she said dawned upon her. She wept for her father. She wept for her brother and for herself.

"Don't cry," begged Edgar. "Don't do crying." He tugged at Gode's arm; but it was no good. And caught up in this scene without fully understanding it, his own eyes brimmed with tears.

Godric looked at the pair of them uneasily. There was nothing he could do; there was nothing he could say.

"I know the fate of the coward," said Gode in a low voice. "My father told me. You may no longer own land, whoever you are; and you can have no lord, you must lay aside laughter and happiness."

Godric shivered involuntarily, unnerved to hear this girl, this daughter of a churl, tell him all he knew so well.

"For all your days you'll be a wanderer," said Gode. Then her voice softened a little; it was as if she was over-awed at the thought, and the meaning of what she had said. "You cannot stay here," she added. "Food you can have, bandage you can have. Then you must go. My father is a man of two hundred shillings; you cannot stay on land he owns."

Godric looked at her with hurt and hatred in his eyes. She had wounded him more with her true words than any weapon could do, far more than the glancing blow of a Danish axe that same afternoon. "Give me the water," he said to Edgar. "I'll wash and bandage myself."

Gode gave him a strip of cloth; and, hardly knowing what she did, for she was spent by emotion, she put aside for him a generous amount of food.

Then Godric stood up and, leaning forward, tipped the rest of the water in the pitcher over his head. He picked up the food after that and, limping a little, walked out of the hut.

In the yard, hampered by his wound, he struggled with great difficulty onto the horse's bare back. The children watched him in silence. Once more he sat astride the gleaming bay, the horse of the prince he had betrayed. He looked down at Gode and Edgar. "Thank you," he said grimly, "for telling me the way."

And with that he spurred the steed, and rode bareback out of the yard.

It was still raining softly, a sad rain from heaven. Gode and Edgar were once more at the entrance to their hut, in and out of which the hens strutted as inclination took them.

The horseman receded into the distance, heading across the blasted land, a rider with nowhere to go.

But Gode was already looking once again to the west, to the backdrop of the distant wood that stood before Maldon. Hopeless, she still hoped. And her brother Edgar sat at her feet, astride the gleaming saddle.

The rain quickened a little and then, quite soon, the curtain of that August day began to fall.

Penelope Lively,
"The Picnic"

One picnic is pretty much like any other, as far as Michael can tell. Gathering up the entire family, heading for some spot "worth seeing," braving the triple threat of wind and wasp and manure to find a place for lunch, maybe enjoying a good rainstorm to top things off. So it is with this trip to the site, in Cornwall, of three Bronze Age stone circles of uncertain origin and purpose, the Hurlers. The day's slide into the absolutely ordinary is hastened by a request from Michael's mother to fetch some forgotten items from the car; but here the predictability ends, as the brutal past that Michael associates with the stone circles reasserts itself. Penelope Lively's stories consider the effects of a place's past sharing time with its present. Here only Michael becomes aware of that occurrence, which has the texture of a dream but is clearly something more by story's end. The conflict between the safe, predictable, and often boring pace of life and an unexpected but once commonplace savagery shapes this story and leaves Michael questioning its closing courtesies.

The Picnic
by Penelope Lively

I HATE PICNICS. There's all this fuss about finding a nice place, and then when you've found it there'll be too much wind, or wasps, or a cow pat, and when everybody's settled down you can be sure something they can't do without will have been left in the car, half a mile away. And it'll be me that's got to go back and get it because I'm the eldest. "Just pop back and get the rug, Michael—it won't take you a minute—and while you're there you might get Jamie's windbreaker, and Dad's pipe, and my glasses, and the baby's bottle . . ."

I hate picnics.

Our picnics are usually to celebrate something. We're a ceremonial family: anniversaries of this, that, and the other; birthdays—even down to the dog's—nothing gets left out. This was Jamie's birthday. Eight. And Jamie, of course, has to pick Bodmin Moor.

"Draughty," said Gran. "I'll stop home in the garden, if nobody minds."

But they weren't having any of that, the parents. We're a united family too: positively tribal. One goes, we all go. "Nonsense," said Mum. "It's not going to be drafty in June. Middle of the summer, you couldn't ask for better." "The Summer Solstice, in fact," said Dad, with his pocket diary open. And then we get a great long disquisition, for Jamie and Gran, about how the solstices are the time of year between the equinoxes when the sun is farthest from the equator and appears to stand still. Yawn, yawn.

And so we fetched up at the Hurlers at half-past eleven on Jamie's birthday, picnic baskets in hand, dog on lead, baby in pram, sun shoved firmly behind a black wodge of cloud and likely to stay there as far as I could see. Lovely picnic weather.

Gran thought it was a funny place to choose for a picnic. "Too bare. And it's industrial. All those chimneys."

I put her right about the chimneys—quietly, not to get anyone upset. "Does being historic tin-mines make them look nicer?" she said, and we had a bit of a giggle about that. She's all right, Gran. But of course it wasn't the tin mines we'd come to see. They're great on having an objective, the parents. We never just go anywhere—we go there to see something. Though in this case, as usual, old Mum gave it one quick look and then was off getting settled in. Finding a nice place out of the wind, somewhere for the pram, a bit of dry grass to sit on, all that. . . .

The Hurlers aren't all that much to look at, granted. A bit stumpy, the stones are, sticking up out of the gorse and stuff—in fact at first they seem just accidental, so that it comes as a bit of a jolt when you realize they are in fact arranged in circles. Even so, they're not on nodding terms with Stonehenge and that lot. We all dealt with them in our own way: Mum didn't bother, Gran had a look round, found herself a nice comfy one to lean against and got her knitting out, Jamie climbed three of them and jumped off again, Toby (the dog) lifted his leg against the biggest and then went rabbiting, Dad held forth to me because nobody else was listening.

"Prehistoric."

"Yes, Dad. How old?" Politely.

That had him floored, as I knew it would, so I told him, because as a matter of fact I'd looked them up in the Cornwall book at school, the day before. "Bronze Age, they think, but nobody's all that sure exactly when. The Beaker People or the Urn People or one of those lots."

"Taken over now by the Picnic People," said Dad. Not all that good a joke, but we enjoyed it until Mum called out—wait for it—that she'd left the newspaper and the baby's feeder in the car and would Michael just pop back for it.

So off I trailed. Mind, it wasn't that far—I've known worse. You could see the car, and the other one that had been there when we'd come. Mum was annoyed about that—she likes having places to herself. We're a territorial family too. She gave it a few nasty looks, but when we got up to the stone circles the other people were some way away, camped on the rising ground nearer the Cheesewring, with *their* picnic and *their* folding stools and *their* rugs and cameras and newspapers.

"That's all right," said Mum. "They're nowhere near. And they look nice." Mum's an expert in niceness. It conducts itself for her, like electricity. She knows if people moving into our street are nice before they've got the removal van unloaded.

"Anyway," said Gran, "you like to know there's someone else around. You don't want to be on your own, do you, not really?"

"Why not?" said Jamie.

"Well—if one of us had an accident or something . . ."

"Listen to you!" said Mum. "I thought this was a celebration."

Coming back from the car, I had a bit of a think about

the stone circles, and what they were for, and all that. Which nobody really knows, of course. *Of religious significance,* the book said, vaguely, and then it waffled on a bit about rites and rituals, meaning, I suppose, that it hadn't a clue really. Of course it's a ritual—any fool can see that. Just like you draw squares on the beach and play hopscotch in them. But what ritual? You couldn't guess hopscotch from the squares, not in a hundred years. There was a slightly gruesome bit in the book about the bones of sacrifices being found near similar stone circles on Dartmoor, and a lot about tribal warfare, which made you realize that it must have been more than somewhat dicey living in those days. It's bad enough now, with cars zooming at you and pollution and all that, but at least I know Mr. Davidson next door isn't likely to stick a knife in me.

I was wrapped in thought, as they say (they actually do —"Wrapped in thought, Michael?" Dad says. Mind, he's got a point, I daresay—it's something I'm known for and apparently it can be more than a bit irritating), and dawdling, I suppose. When I looked back at the Hurlers I could see Mum standing up waving. Hurry up, she meant, not hello, how nice to see you again. It was twelve exactly, my watch said—I hadn't been gone that long— but I ran a bit, or at least I trotted because I'm in favor of a quiet life and Mum can get antsy if she's kept waiting.

I tripped over a stone or something once, and came down a cropper on the grass. Just as I got up, the sun came out. At least it came out in one place but not in another, if you see what I mean, so that where I was it was still gray and dull but over there at the Hurlers, and beyond, all the way up the slope beyond, it was bright sun. Funny. You could see the shafts of sunshine streaming down onto Mum and the rest of them, and the other family in their picnic place. I could see them very clearly, all standing or sitting quite still, as though they were kind of frozen by sun, I thought. Silly idea.

And then the wodge of cloud plonked itself back again and it went gray. I arrived at where the family were and gave Mum the paper and the feeder, but she seemed abstracted. She didn't even say thank you, which was odd, because one thing you can say is that Mum's got nice manners. Outside the family as well as in. Everybody likes Mum. She'd got the picnic all laid out but she was staring over towards the other family all the time.

We sat down and Mum began dishing out sandwiches. After a minute she said, "You know, they've moved. They've come a bit nearer."

And Dad said, "Yes, I think they have." He was staring too.

I looked. They'd put themselves into a bit where the gorse made a windbreak, the other family.

There was a pause. Mum was unscrewing Thermoses. And then all of a sudden she said, "They've got no business."

I looked at her. Her voice sounded most peculiar— kind of strangled. She really meant it. She minded.

"Oh, come on, Mum," I said. "They've got as much right here as us." She took no notice of that and what's more, neither did anyone else. They were all looking over at the other family. Gran had put down her knitting and was muttering to herself. It was extraordinary.

They weren't eating yet, the other family. You could see all their stuff, in baskets and that, but they hadn't unpacked it. There were four of them—parents and two kids, around eleven or twelve, and the inevitable dog.

And then while we were looking at them they got up and wandered off up the slope, as though maybe they were going up to the Cheesewring. Before they went they all stared over at us. It seemed to be catching, this business.

We ate our sandwiches, and drank our tea, and nobody said anything much. Not even Jamie. Once Dad asked if there was anything more to eat. "No," said Mum. "That's the lot. Sorry. I should have brought more." Once or twice I tried to jolly things up a bit, but nobody was having any.

And then all of a sudden Mum said, "Jamie. See if you can get some of their sandwiches."

Once upon a time, a long time ago, when Jamie was about four, he nicked a brass screw from Woolworth's. He thought you could help yourself, you see—all those nice trays with shiny things in them. And Mum just about went through the roof. She took it back to the manager herself, personally, and Jamie had to come, too, so he'd know what was what forever and ever about taking things that aren't yours.

I thought I couldn't have heard right. I gaped at her with my mouth open like someone in a bad TV film.

Not so Jamie. "Okay," he said. And he got up and went off through the gorse and stones and bushes toward the other family's picnic place. He went off, I say, but he went in a way I'd never seen him go before. He kind of slid from bush to bush and stone to stone, rather like he'd do if he was playing stalking, or tracking, or like I did when I was his age. Only he was doing it properly. Professionally, as it were. As though he'd been doing it all his life. Most of the time I couldn't see him at all, myself, even though I knew where he was. He melted, somehow, from one place to the next.

I watched, not saying anything because I was still too shocked to say anything. And the others watched, but they weren't shocked. Just interested. "Good boy," said Gran, once. "Good lad."

I took off my glasses and scrubbed them around on my sleeve. It's a thing I do when I'm fussed about something. You always feel as though things might clear up if you can see better. But even when I could see the moor unsmudged and unspotted, Jamie was still tracking over to that patch of rug on the hillside, and the parents and Gran were still sitting there watching him, cool as cucumbers.

The other family stopped and looked back once or twice. It was almost as though they had a feeling there might be something going on. But every time they looked Jamie melted into a stone or a bush, and they didn't seem to see him.

And then he darted at their basket, whipped something out, and was gone again, so quick it hardly seemed to have happened.

He got back. With half a dozen sandwiches wrapped in silver foil. "Ham," said Mum. "Nice. Bread's from a cut loaf, though." She passed them round. Everyone took one except me. I said I wasn't hungry, thank you.

"Anything wrong, Michael?" said Mum, quite ordinary and calm. "It's not like you to turn food down."

I said angrily, "Of course there's something wrong. I don't know what you . . ." But they weren't paying me any attention.

"What else have they got, Jamie?" said Dad.

"Bananas. Some cans of Coke. Tart things—shop ones. Lyons, I think."

"Not worth it," said Mum. "Anyway, they're coming back."

They were walking quite fast down the slope now, the other family, back to their things. It was overcast now. Gray, chilly. It felt as though it might rain.

I said, "Let's go home. It's going to rain."

"What?" said Mum. Not meaning, "I didn't hear you," but "I'm not listening to you."

The baby started fussing. Mum reached into the picnic basket and gave her a chicken bone.

If I hadn't seen it with my own eyes, I'd never have believed it. Pampered, that baby's been, from birth. Orange juice, strained messes, sterilized this and that.

As soon as Mum wasn't looking I took the chicken bone away. And the baby started yelling so I had to give it back. I took my glasses off again and had another scrub round the lenses.

The other family had got back to their place. They sat down on their folding chairs and on the rug, half out of sight now behind some bushes, though the father seemed to have put himself deliberately so that he faced out toward us. Presently, though, he moved, and we couldn't see any of them—just a corner of the rug.

We were on a grassy bit at the top end of the stone circle. Mum had picked it for flatness and absence of gorse, after a slight argument with Gran, who had wanted to stay by her personal choice of stone. Now Dad said all of a sudden, "It won't do, here."

So they were seeing sense at last. "No," I said. "And it is raining now, anyway. Let's get off home."

"What do you mean, Michael? Don't be silly," said Mum. And then she said to Dad, "You're right. Too enclosed. You can't see the approaches."

Gran and Jamie had joined in now. They were on about cover, and that line of scrub over there, and having someone on the higher ground as a lookout. I just sat there. It was like a bad dream. And the rain was serious now.

"Come on," said Mum. And suddenly there we all were, collecting everything up—Thermoses, rugs, the lot —and moving them into a place just beyond the stone circle where there was a hollow in the ground and, just above it, a crest with whortle bushes and stuff. The bushes hid the hollow from the opposite slope. Dad lay on his stomach and stared through the bushes for a moment.

"Fine," he said. "Good view of their site, but they can't see us."

"They'll have a lookout," said Mum.

"True enough."

I said, "Look, I don't know what's the matter with everybody. They're just another family, those other people. *Another family.* Like us."

"Don't shout so, dear," said Mum.

"Should get one of them," said Gran.

"Hostage?"

"Maybe. We'll see."

Or else I'd gone barmy. Stark, raving mad. There they all were, sitting in the rain, looking out through the bushes every now and then, and going on like this. That was another thing—sitting there in the rain. We're a rain-allergic family, we are. One gray cloud on the horizon and we strike camp. Two drops and we're off the beach for the day. A doubtful weather-forecast and we stay at home. And there they were just sitting with the rain running off them, taking no more notice than a lot of horses in a field would.

I said, "I'm getting wet."

"What?" said Mum. "What" meaning "Don't bother me" again.

"I know," I said, all bright and breezy. "It's a game. It's some sort of joke you thought up between you while I was down at the car. Jolly funny. But let's stop now."

Nobody paid the slightest attention.

"Shh," said Jamie. "I can hear something. . . ."

I couldn't. At least only birds and the usual kind of outdoor noises. And the rain.

"Downwind," said Dad. "There's one of them coming downwind."

They were all staring through the bushes now, lying on their stomachs. "It's one of the children," said Mum. "I saw a bit of jersey just then."

Dad slid back into the hollow and rummaged around in the grass. He picked up a lump of stone, fist sized, and then he stood up, looked quickly around, and threw it. Then he ducked down again.

There was a kind of gasp, from not far away. The noise you make when you've stubbed your toe or something.

"Got him," said Dad.

"That'll teach 'em," said Gran.

"Stop it. . . ." I said. I was almost in tears, I can tell you.

"Be quiet, Michael. Raid, do you think, or full-scale attack?"

"Raid," said Dad. "He's going back."

I said, in a silly, high-pitched voice, because I was getting in such a fuss I hardly knew if I was coming or going, "If you do that kind of thing to people, they're likely to do it back to you." I sounded like Mum, when I was three or four, and having a spat with one of my mates. "Oh, *please* can't we go home," I said, since nobody so much as listened to that one. And I looked at my watch.

It said twelve exactly. But it had said that a quarter of an hour or so ago, when I was coming back from the car, so I listened to it. It hadn't stopped, at least only the hands had. I shook it, but the hands stayed stuck. It's a rotten watch, anyway: seven and a half books of Green Shield stamps. "Where's Toby?" said Jamie, suddenly.

Mum humped herself up to the top of the ridge, very cautious, and whistled. He always comes best for Mum. Knows where the food supply is.

Nothing happened. No Toby bouncing through the grass. Mum knelt up so that she could see better and whistled again.

And a stone whizzed past her ear and thumped down onto the rug.

"Get down!" said Dad.

"They've got within range, somehow!"

"We'll have to move."

"Not if I can find out where he is," said Dad grimly.

He went up on the ridge, and stood, and then ducked. At once another stone flew past him and smack into the side of the pram.

"Behind that big rock over there. Only one of them."

They were all grubbing around for stones. "Come on, Michael," said Mum. "Don't just leave everything to everyone else."

I grubbed, miserably, and found a bit of granite and then lost it again. The rest of them had got a good supply, including Gran. She was getting together a nice little store.

"I'm going to winkle him out," said Dad. He was filling his anorak pockets with stones. "Have we got a knife?" Casually.

"Dad!" I said. At least I meant to. It came out as a sort of squeak.

"Only the plastic ones," said Mum.

"Pity. I'll have one of them, all the same."

He went out of the hollow the back way, as it were, and for a minute or two we could hear him rustling along from bush to bush. Then silence for what seemed a long time.

Then a grunt, crashing noises, a yell, someone running, more thumps. And Dad came back, panting, a dirty great swelling on the side of his cheek.

"Sent him packing!"

Nobody but me paid any attention to the bruise.

I said, "Did he do that?"

"What? Oh, he clipped me with a stone before I could get to him."

Mum didn't even look at it. Mum, who's brandishing the antiseptic and the plaster around at the merest hint of a scratch, normally.

"Which of them was it?"

"Young one, again. The rest have stayed put."

"Now what?"

"Now we go home," I said, hopelessly.

"I reckon," said Dad, "we use Jamie as a decoy. Try to draw one or two of them off, and then go in. Drive them back up the hill."

"What about me?" said Gran.

"You stay here. You and the baby. Retreat if you have to."

Gran nodded.

"Why did you have to interfere with them in the first place?" I shouted. "If you'd just left them alone all this wouldn't be happening."

Mum stared at me. "They'd got things we wanted, hadn't they?" she said. "Do get on and collect some stones, Michael. I don't know what's got into you today."

Dad was explaining things to Jamie. He was to get out of the hollow and work his way around till he was on the far side of their site, and then he was to attract their attention, show himself, and make off fast. With any luck one or two of them would come out after him.

"Look," I said. "He might get *hurt*. If they're carrying on like this too. You can *kill* people, throwing stones."

"Then we'll have to hurt them back, won't we?" said Dad, reasonably.

"But we've only got to go somewhere else. . . ."

"Our place," said Gran. "Got to keep it. Silly boy."

There wasn't any point in going on.

Jamie was getting ready to slip away. "Don't be long," said Mum. I looked at my watch; reflex action. Still stuck at twelve; still ticking. Stupid cheap watch.

And just as Jamie wriggled through the first few yards of cover it happened. A whole hail of stones, banging down on the rug and the Thermoses and the grass. "Take cover behind the chairs," said Dad to Gran. "The rest of you up on the ridge."

We flattened out along the top, clutching stones. Thirty yards away or so a head came out from behind a slab of rock. A stone came flying toward us, and fell short. There was movement in several different places.

"It's all of them," said Dad. "Michael, you look after that one on the right."

I threw a stone in that direction, halfheartedly. It bounced off a rock. And just as I'd got my head down again one came back and caught me on the arm. It hurt. And suddenly I wanted to do it back to somebody, like when you're about five. I took the biggest stone I could see from the pile behind us that Gran was busy stoking up all the time, and I stood up and chucked it at something red I could see beyond the next big boulder. Meaning not to miss, that time.

And somebody yelled.

"Good shot!" said Dad.

That made me see sense again.

"Stop it!" I yelled. "Look, just stop it, all of you!" And I slid back down off the ridge. I wasn't having any more to do with it.

Gran was sitting on the grass behind the folding chairs, with the baby beside her. The baby was watching what she was doing and making the daft "Ooo" and "Aaa" noises that babies make (rather nice, in fact, but I was in too much of a state to stop and have a chat like I would normally). What she was doing, Gran, was making a fire out of paper bags and dry grass (it kept going out, of course, because of the rain) and putting chicken bones on it and kind of mumbling at it. Barmy. Just clean, honest-to-goodness barmy. No wonder the baby was interested.

There wasn't time, though, to ask her what precisely she thought she was doing because first Jamie gave a yell and said, "Oh, look, look!" and started waving Toby's collar around, which had come hurtling onto the ground beside us tied onto a stone, and then pebbles and things were coming down so thick and fast that Dad and Mum came sliding down and Dad said, "Out! Get out, all of you. Back to the circle, and into the gorse beyond."

Jamie was wailing, "They've got Toby!" and Gran was chanting away now at her stupid fire, for all the world like somebody in church, until Dad bundled her up and off, and we were all scuttling over the grass, dragging things with us.

"Stop!" said Dad, and they all got down behind a big lump of granite on the edge of the circle. Not me, though.

"Michael! I said *stop*—come back here!"

"No." I'd had enough. I began to run, the wet grass snatching at my feet so that I tripped and I could hear Dad yelling still, and Mum, but I got up again and went on. I could see the car and that was where I was going. After that I didn't care. I wasn't staying another minute in that stupid, crazy place with everyone behaving like lunatics.

I ran, with whatever I'd picked up (the newspaper and the baby's feeder, of all things) clutched in one hand, and the rain streaming down on my face. I couldn't hear them anymore. Nothing. Just me, panting, and birds and things.

I fell over again. I think I banged my head or something, because for some reason I didn't get up at once. I lay there facedown for a minute, heaving and blowing, and expecting someone to throw a stone at me, or jump on me.

I lifted my head and I could see them, Mum and Dad and Jamie and Gran and the baby. They were sitting about in the middle of the stone circle, and the sun had come out. They were just sitting in the sun. And Mum was waving.

I arrived at where they were and Mum took the paper and the feeder.

"Thanks, dear. What's the matter?"

"Nothing," I said.

"You didn't have to rush so. It's only just gone twelve."

It had, that stupid watch said so. About thirty seconds past.

"What were you doing?" said Mum. "Just lying on the grass there?"

"Wrapped in thought, eh?" said Dad.

"There's something wrong with my watch."

"Let's see."

"It doesn't matter," I said. "It's going again now."

"And it was raining down there," said Mum. "We could see. You've let yourself get soaked."

"When are we having my birthday picnic?" said Jamie.

Mum started dishing out the sandwiches. The sun was out; the baby had gone to sleep; Dad was reading the paper. All right, I've got a vivid imagination. It's not a crime.

"There's someone coming," I said.

"No need to sound so put out," said Mum. "It's just one of that other family."

"He's got Toby," said Jamie.

"So he has."

The man had his tie knotted round Toby's neck. "This little chap belong to you, by any chance?"

"He's slipped his collar," said Jamie. "*Bad* dog."

"That's very kind of you," said Mum. "We're most grateful. Thank you very much."

"Not at all. Wonder if I might ask you a favor, in fact. Loan of a can opener for five minutes."

Mum was rummaging in the picnic basket.

"Exchange is no robbery," said Dad.

"Fair enough," said the man. "Seems to be turning out fine after all."

"Lovely."

Mum found the can opener.

"Very kind of you. Spoils the day a bit if you can't get at the food."

"There's always something," said Mum.

"Too right. We already had one of the kids get in an argument with a rock."

"My husband's just had a bit of a fall. Nothing much."

It was the first time I'd noticed the swelling on the side of Dad's face.

"Dangerous place," said the man.

Everybody was smiling away, except me.

Nicholasa Mohr,
"A Very Special Pet"

Isolation is a common theme in fiction and in the life it reflects. Individuals struggle to overcome certain barriers, to gain acceptance, or to establish a place for themselves. Although isolated, Graciela Fernández is not part of any such struggle. She has chosen to confine herself to her family's small apartment in the Bronx, having experienced fear on the city's subways and crowded streets. Caught in a depressing present, Mrs. Fernández is also cut off from her past—their tiny mountain village in Puerto Rico and a way of life closer to the land—and left with little hope for the future. Her attempt to change the situation, however briefly, is unsuccessful, leaving her with nothing more than a familiar song about a beautiful tropical island.

A Very Special Pet
by Nicholasa Mohr

THE FERNÁNDEZ FAMILY kept two pets in their small five-room apartment. One was a large female alley cat who was a good mouser when she wasn't in heat. She was very large and had a rich coat of gray fur with black stripes and a long bushy tail. Her eyes were yellow and she had long white whiskers. Her name was Maríalu.

If they would listen carefully to what Maríalu said, Mrs. Fernández assured the children, they would hear her calling her husband Raúl.

"Raúl . . . Raúl . . . this is Maríalu . . . Raúl . . . Raúl . . . this is Maríalu," the children would sing loudly. They all felt sorry for Maríalu, because no matter how long and hard she howled, or how many times she ran off, she could never find her real husband, Raúl.

The second pet was not really supposed to be a pet at all. She was a small, skinny white hen with a red crest and a yellow beak. Graciela and Eugenio Fernández had bought her two years ago, to provide them and their eight children with good fresh eggs.

Her name was Joncrofo, after Graciela Fernández's favorite Hollywood movie star, Joan Crawford. People would repeat the hen's name as she pronounced it, "Joncrofo la gallina."

Joncrofo la gallina lived in the kitchen. She had one foot tied with a very long piece of twine to one of the legs of the kitchen sink. The twine was long enough for Joncrofo to wander all over the kitchen and even to hop onto the large window with the fire escape. Under the sink

Mrs. Fernández kept clean newspapers, water, and corn-meal for the hen, and a wooden box lined with some soft flannel cloth and packing straw. It was there that they hoped Joncrofo would lay her eggs. The little hen slept and rested there, but perhaps because she was nervous, she had never once laid an egg.

Graciela and Eugenio Fernández had come to the Bronx six years ago and moved into the small apartment. Except for a trip once before to the seaport city of Maya-güez in Puerto Rico, they had never left their tiny village in the mountains. To finance their voyage to New York, Mr. and Mrs. Fernández had sold their small plot of land, the little livestock they had, and their wooden cabin. The sale had provided the fare and expenses for them and their five children. Since then, three more chil-dren had been born. City life was foreign to them, and they had to learn everything, even how to get on a sub-way and travel. Graciela Fernández had been terribly frightened at first of the underground trains, traffic, and large crowds of people. Although she finally adjusted, she still confined herself to the apartment and seldom went out.

She would never complain; she would pray at the small altar she had set up in the kitchen, light her candles, and murmur that God would provide and not forget her and her family. She was proud of the fact that they did not have to ask for welfare or home relief, as so many other families did.

"Papi provides for us. We are lucky and we have to thank Jesus Christ," she would say, making the sign of the cross.

Eugenio Fernández had found a job as a porter in one of the large buildings in the garment center in Manhattan. He still held the same job, but he hoped to be promoted someday to freight-elevator operator. In the meantime he sold newspapers and coffee on the side, ran errands for people in the building, and was always available for extra work. Still, the money he brought home was barely enough to support ten people.

"Someday I'm gonna get that job. I got my eye on it, and Mr. Friedlander, he likes me . . . so we gotta be patient. Besides the increase in salary, my God!—I could do a million things on the side, and we could make a lotta money. Why I could . . ." Mr. Fernández would tell his family this story several times a week.

"Oh, wow! Papi, we are gonna be rich when you get that job!" the children would shriek.

"Can we get a television when we get rich, Papi?" Pablito, the oldest boy, would ask. Nellie, Carmen, and Linda wanted a telephone.

"Everybody on the block got a telephone but us." Nellie, the oldest girl, would speak for them.

The younger children, William, Olgita, and Freddie, would request lots of toys and treats. Baby Nancy would smile and babble happily with everybody.

"We gonna get everything and we gonna leave El Bronx," Mr. Fernández would assure them. "We even gonna save enough to buy our farm in Puerto Rico—a big one! With lots of land, maybe a hundred acres, and a chicken house, pigs, goats, even a cow. We can plant coffee and some sugar, and have all the fruit trees— mangoes, sweet oranges, everything!" Mr. Fernández would pause and tell the children all about the wonderful food they could eat back home in his village. "All you need to get the farm is a good start."

"We gonna take Joncrofo, right?" the kids would ask. "And Maríalu? Her too?"

"Sure," Mr. Fernández would say good-naturedly, "even Raúl, her husband, when she finds him, eh?" He would wink, laughing. "And Joncrofo don't have to be tied up like a prisoner no more—she could run loose."

It was the dream of Graciela and Eugenio Fernández to go back to their village as owners of their own farm, with the faith that the land would provide for them.

This morning Mrs. Fernández sat in her kitchen, thinking that things were just not going well. Now that the holidays were coming and Christmas would soon be here, money was scarcer than ever and prices were higher than ever. Things had been hard for Eugenio Fernández; he was still working as a porter and lately had been sick with a bad throat. They had not saved one cent toward their farm. In fact, they still owed the dry-goods salesman for the kitchen curtains and two bedspreads; even insurance payments were long overdue. She wanted to find a job and help out, but there were still three small preschool children at home to care for. Lately, she had begun to worry; it was hard to put meat on the table.

Graciela Fernández sighed, looking about her small, clean kitchen, and caught sight of Joncrofo running frantically after a stray cockroach. The hen quickly jerked her neck and snapped up the insect with her beak. In spite of all the fumigation and daily scrubbing, it seemed there was always a cockroach or two in sight. Joncrofo was always searching for a tasty morsel—spiders, ants, even houseflies. She was quick and usually got her victim.

The little white hen had a wicked temper and would snap at anyone she felt was annoying her. Even Maríalu knew better; she had a permanent scar on her right ear as a result of Joncrofo's sharp yellow beak. Now the cat carefully kept her distance.

In spite of Joncrofo's cantankerous ways, the children loved her. They were proud of her because no one else on the block had such a pet. Whenever other children teased them about not having a television, the Fernández children would remind them that Joncrofo was a very special pet. Even Baby Nancy would laugh and clap when she saw Joncrofo rushing toward one of her tiny victims.

For some time now Mrs. Fernández had given up any hope of Joncrofo producing eggs and had also accepted her as a house pet. She had tried everything: warm milk, fresh grass from the park, relining the wooden box. She had even consulted the spiritualist and followed the instructions faithfully, giving the little hen certain herbs to eat and reciting the prayers; and yet nothing ever worked. She had even tried to fatten her up, but the more Joncrofo ate, it seemed, the less she gained.

After thinking about it for several days, this morning Graciela Fernández reached her decision. Tonight, her husband would have good fresh chicken broth for his cold, and her children a full plate of rice with chicken. This silly hen was really no use alive to anyone, she concluded.

It had been six long years since Mrs. Fernández had killed a chicken, but she still remembered how. She was grateful that the older children were in school, and somehow she would find a way to keep the three younger ones at the other end of the apartment.

Very slowly she got up and found the kitchen cleaver. Feeling it with her thumb, she decided it should be sharper, and taking a flat stone, she carefully sharpened the edge as she planned the best way to finish off the hen.

It was still quite early. If she worked things right, she could be through by noontime and have supper ready before her husband got home. She would tell the children that Joncrofo flew away. Someone had untied the twine on her foot and when she opened the window to the fire escape to bring in the mop, Joncrofo flew out and disappeared. That's it, she said to herself, satisfied.

The cleaver was sharp enough and the small chopping block was set up on the kitchen sink. Mrs. Fernández bent down and looked Joncrofo right in the eye. The hen stared back without any fear or much interest. Good, thought Mrs. Fernández, and she walked back into the apartment where Olgita, Freddie, and Baby Nancy were playing.

"I'm going to clean the kitchen, and I don't want you to come inside. Understand?" The children looked at her and nodded. "I mean it—you stay here. If I catch you coming to the kitchen when I am cleaning, you get it with this," she said, holding out her hand with an open palm, gesturing as if she were spanking them. "Now, I'm going to put the chair across the kitchen entrance so that Baby Nancy can't come in. Okay?" The children nodded again. Their mother very often put one of the kitchen chairs across the kitchen entrance so the baby could not come inside. "Now," she said, "you listen and you stay here!" The children began to play, interested only in their game.

Mrs. Fernández returned to the kitchen, smoothed down her hair, readjusted her apron, and rolled up her sleeves. She put one of the chairs across the threshold to block the entrance, then found a couple of extra rags and old newspapers.

"Joncrofo," she whispered, and walked over to the hen. To her surprise, the hen ran under the sink and sat in her box. Mrs. Fernández bent down, but before she could grab her, Joncrofo jumped out of her box and slid behind one of the legs of the kitchen sink. She extended her hand and felt the hen's sharp beak nip one of her fingers. "Ave María!" she said, pulling away and putting the injured finger in her mouth. "Okay, you wanna play games. You dumb hen!"

She decided to untie the twine that was tied to the leg of the sink and then pull the hen toward her. Taking a large rag, she draped it over one hand and then, bending down once more, untied the twine and began to pull. Joncrofo resisted, and Mrs. Fernández pulled. Harder and harder she tugged and pulled, at the same time making sure she held the rag securely, so that she could protect herself against Joncrofo's sharp beak. Quickly she pulled, and with one fast jerk of the twine, the hen was up in the air. Quickly Mrs. Fernández draped the rag over the hen. Frantically, Joncrofo began to cackle and jump, flapping her wings and snapping her beak. Mrs. Fernández found herself spinning as she struggled to hold on to Joncrofo, who kept wriggling and jumping. With great effort Joncrofo got her head loose and sank her beak into Mrs. Fernández's arm. In an instant she released the hen.

Joncrofo ran around the kitchen cackling loudly, flapping her wings and ruffling her feathers. The hen kept an eye on Mrs. Fernández, who also watched her as she held on to her injured arm. White feathers were all over the kitchen; some still floated softly in the air.

Each time Mrs. Fernández went toward Joncrofo, she fled swiftly, cackling even louder and snapping wildly with her beak.

Mrs. Fernández remained still for a moment, then went over to the far end of the kitchen and grabbed a broom. Using the handle, she began to hit the hen, swatting her back and forth like a tennis ball. Joncrofo kept running and trying to dodge the blows, but Mrs. Fernández kept landing the broom each time. The hen began to lose her footing, and Mrs. Fernández vigorously swung the broom, hitting the small white hen until her cackles became softer and softer. Not able to stand any longer, Joncrofo wobbled, moving with slow jerky movements, and dropped to the floor. Mrs. Fernández let go of the broom and rushed over to the hen. Grabbing her by the neck, she lifted her into the air and spun her around a few times, dropping her on the floor. Near exhaustion, Mrs. Fernández could hear her own heavy breathing.

"Mami . . . Mamita. What are you doing to Joncrofo?" Turning, she saw Olgita, Freddie, and Baby Nancy staring at her wide eyed. "Ma . . . Mami . . . what are you doing to Joncrofo?" they shouted and began to cry. In her excitement, Mrs. Fernández had forgotten completely about the children and the noise the hen had made.

"Oooo . . . is she dead?" Olgita cried, pointing. "Is she dead?" She began to whine.

"You killed Joncrofo, Mami! You killed her. She's dead." Freddie joined his sister, sobbing loudly. Baby Nancy watched her brother and sister and began to cry too. Shrieking, she threw herself on the floor in a tantrum.

"You killed her! You're bad, Mami. You're bad," screamed Olgita.

"Joncrofo . . . I want Joncrofo. . . ." Freddie sobbed. "I'm gonna tell Papi," he screamed, choking with tears.

"Me too! I'm gonna tell too," cried Olgita. "I'm telling Nellie, and she'll tell her teacher on you," she yelled.

Mrs. Fernández watched her children as they stood looking in at her, barricaded by the chair. Then she looked down at the floor where Joncrofo lay, perfectly still. Walking over to the chair, she removed it from the entrance, and before she could say anything, the children ran to the back of the apartment, still yelling and crying.

"Joncrofo. . . . We want Joncrofo. . . . You're bad . . . you're bad. . . ."

Mrs. Fernández felt completely helpless as she looked about her kitchen. What a mess! she thought. Things were overturned, and there were white feathers everywhere. Feeling the tears coming to her eyes, she sat down and began to cry quietly. What's the use now? She sighed and thought, I should have taken her to the butcher. He would have done it for a small fee. Oh, this life, she said to herself, wiping her eyes. Now my children hate me. She remembered that when she was just about Olgita's age she was already helping her mother kill chickens and never thought much about slaughtering animals for food.

Graciela Fernández took a deep breath and began to wonder what she would do with Joncrofo now that she was dead. No use cooking her. They won't eat her, she thought, shaking her head. As she contemplated what was to be done, she heard a low grunt. Joncrofo was still alive!

Mrs. Fernández reached under the sink and pulled out

the wooden box. She put the large rag into the box and placed the hen inside. Quickly she went over to a cabinet and took out an eyedropper, filling it with water. Then she forced open Joncrofo's beak and dropped some water inside. She put a washcloth into lukewarm water and washed down the hen, smoothing her feathers.

"Joncrofo," she cooed softly, "cro . . . cro . . . Joncrofita," and stroked the hen gently. The hen was still breathing, but her eyes were closed. Mrs. Fernández went over to the cupboard and pulled out a small bottle of rum that Mr. Fernández saved only for special occasions and for guests. She gave some to Joncrofo. The hen opened her eyes and shook her head, emitting a croaking sound.

"What a good little hen," said Mrs. Fernández. "That's right, come on . . . come, wake up, and I'll give you something special. How about if I get you some nice dried corn? . . . Come on." She continued to pet the hen and talk sweetly to her. Slowly, Joncrofo opened her beak and tried to cackle, and again she made a croaking sound. Blinking her eyes, she sat up in her box, ruffled her feathers, and managed a low soft cackle.

"Is she gonna live, Mami?" Mrs. Fernández turned and saw Olgita, Freddie, and Baby Nancy standing beside her.

"Of course she's going to live. What did you think I did, kill her? Tsk, tsk . . . did you really think that? You are all very silly children," she said, and shook her finger at them. They stared back at her with bewilderment, not speaking. "All that screaming at me was not nice." She went on, "I was only trying to save her. Joncrofo got very sick, and see?" She held up the eyedropper. "I had to help her get well. I had to catch her in order to cure her. Understand?"

Olgita and Freddie looked at each other and then at their mother.

"When I saw that she was getting sick, I had to catch her. She was running all around, jumping and going crazy. Yes." Mrs. Fernández opened her eyes and pointed to her head, making a circular movement with her right index finger. "She went cuckoo! If I didn't stop her, Joncrofo would have really killed herself," she said earnestly. "So I gave her some medicine—and now . . ."

"Is that why you got her drunk, Mami?" interrupted Olgita.

"What?" asked Mrs. Fernández.

"You gave her Papi's rum . . . in the eyedropper. We seen you," Freddie said. Olgita nodded.

"Well," Mrs. Fernández said, "that don't make her drunk. It . . . it . . . ah . . . just calms her down. Sometimes it's used like a medicine."

"And makes her happy again?" Olgita asked. "Like Papi? He always gets happy when he drink some."

"Yes, that's right. You're right. To make Joncrofo happy again," Mrs. Fernández said.

"Why did she get sick, Mami, and go crazy?" asked Freddie.

"I don't know why. Those things just happen," Mrs. Fernández responded.

"Do them things happen on the farm in Puerto Rico?"

"That's right," she said. "Now let me be. I gotta finish cleaning here. Go on, go to the back of the house; take Baby Nancy . . . go on."

The children left the kitchen, and Mrs. Fernández barricaded the entrance once more. She picked up the box with Joncrofo, who sat quietly blinking, and shoved it under the sink. Then she put the cleaver and the chopping board away. Picking up the broom, she began to sweep the feathers and torn newspapers that were strewn all about the kitchen.

In the back of the apartment, where the children played, they could hear their mother singing a familiar song. It was about a beautiful island where the tall green palm trees swayed under a golden sky and the flowers were always in bloom.

Joan Aiken, "A Room Full of Leaves"

The enormous family home that Wilfred will inherit when his Uncle Winthrop dies seems to hold the possibility of fantasy along its dark and dusty, near-forgotten passages winding past enough rooms "for each day of the year and plenty left over." Fantasy, however, suggests play, and Wilfred's ever-watchful and wonderfully horrid guardians permit nothing of the sort. Having so much to live up to, Wilfred (or Wil, as he prefers) is not allowed to fritter away his time in play. Quickly seizing a rare opportunity to escape Aunt Agatha, Squabb, and Buckle, Wil loses himself near the back of the house. Here, not quite by chance, he discovers a fabulous room and welcome companion, which then must be protected. Joan Aiken, like Wil a child of a writer, has created a story rich in humor, filled with money-grubbing adults. However, the story is left finally in the hands of two children playing among the branches of a wondrous tree (a family tree, perhaps?).

A Room Full of Leaves

by Joan Aiken

ONCE THERE WAS a poor little boy who lived with a lot of his relatives in an enormous house called Troy. The relatives were rich, but they were so nasty that they might just as well have been poor, for all the good their money did them. The worst of them all was Aunt Agatha, who was thin and sharp, and the next worst was Uncle Umbert, who was stout and prosperous. We shall return to them later. There was also a fierce old nurse called Squabb, and a tutor, Mr. Buckle, who helped to make the little boy's life a burden. His name was Wilfred, which was a family name, but he was so tired of hearing them all say: "You must live up to your name, child," that in his own mind he called himself Wil. It had to be in his mind, for he had no playmates—other children were declared to be common, and probably dangerous and infectious too.

One rainy Saturday afternoon Wil sat in his schoolroom finishing some Latin parsing for Mr. Buckle before being taken for his walk, which was always in one of two directions. If Squabb took him they went downtown "to look at the shops" in a suburb of London which was sprawling out its claws toward the big house; but the shops were never the ones Wil would have chosen to look at. If he went with Mr. Buckle they crossed the Common diagonally (avoiding the pond where rude little boys sailed their boats) and came back along the white-railed ride while Mr. Buckle talked about plant life.

So Wil was not looking forward with great enthusiasm

to his walk, and when Squabb came in and told him that it was too wet to go out and he must amuse himself quietly with his transfers, he was delighted. He sat gazing dreamily at the transfers for a while, not getting on with them, while Squabb did some ironing. It was nearly dark, although the time was only three. Squabb switched on the light and picked a fresh heap of ironing off the fender.

All of a sudden there was a blue flash and a report from the iron; a strong smell of burnt rubber filled the room and all the lights went out.

"Now I suppose the perishing thing's fused all this floor," exclaimed Squabb, and she hurried out of the room, muttering something under her breath about new-fangled gadgets.

Wil did not waste a second. Before the door had closed after her he was tiptoeing across the room and out of the other door. In the darkness and confusion no one would miss him for quite a considerable time, and he would have a rare opportunity to be on his own for a bit.

The house in which he lived was very huge. Nobody knew exactly how many rooms there were—but there was one for each day of the year and plenty left over. Innumerable little courtyards, each with its own patch of green velvet grass, had passages leading away in all directions to different blocks and wings. Toward the back of the house there were fewer courtyards; it drew itself together into a solid mass which touched the forest behind. The most important rooms were open to the public on four days a week; Mr. Buckle and a skinny lady from the town showed visitors round, and all the relics and heirlooms were carefully locked up inside glass cases where they could be gazed at—the silver washbasin used by James II, a dirty old exercise book belonging to the poet

Pope, the little pot of neat's foot ointment left by Henry VIII, and all the other tiny bits of history. Even in those days visitors were careless about leaving things behind.

Wil was indifferent to the public rooms, though his relatives were not. They spent their lives polishing and furbishing and when everything was polished they went on endless grubbing searches through the unused rooms looking for more relics which could be cleaned up and sold to the British Museum.

Wil stood outside the schoolroom door listening. Down below he could hear the murmur of voices. Saturday was cheap visiting day—only two and six instead of five shillings—so there were twice as many people, and both Mr. Buckle and the skinny lady were at work escorting their little groups. Wil nodded to himself and slipped away, softly as a mouse, toward the back of the house where the tourists were never taken. Here it became darker and dustier, the windows were small, heavily leaded, and never cleaned. Little passages, unexpected stairways and landings, wound about past innumerable doors, many of which had not been opened since Anne Boleyn popped her head around to say good-bye to some bedridden old retainer before taking horse to London. Tapestries hung thick with velvet dust—had Wil touched them they would have crumbled to pieces but he slid past them like a shadow.

He was already lost, but he meant to be; he stood listening to the old house creaking and rustling around him like a forest. He had a fancy that if he penetrated far enough he would find himself in the forest without having noticed the transition. He was following a particularly crooked and winding passage, leading to a kind of crossroads or cross-passages from which other alleys led away, mostly dark, some with a faint gleam from a rain-streaked window far away down their length, and all lined with doors.

He paused, wondering which to choose, and then heard something which might have been the faintest of whispers—but it was enough to decide him on taking the passage directly fronting him. He went slowly to a door some twelve feet along it, rather a low, small door on his right.

After pushing he discovered that it opened outward toward him. He pulled it back, stepped around, and gazed in bewilderment at what he saw. It was like a curtain, of a silvery, faded brown, which hung across the doorway. Then looking closer he saw that it was really *leaves*—piled high and drifted one on another, lying so heaped up that the entrance was filled with them, and if the door had swung inward he could never have pushed it open. Wil felt them with his hand; they were not brittle like dead beech-leaves, but soft and supple, making only the faintest rustle when he touched them. He took one and looked at it in the palm of his hand. It was almost a skeleton, covered with faint silvery marks like letters. As he stood looking at it he heard a little voice whisper from inside the room:

"Well, boy, aren't you coming in?"

Much excited, he stared once more at the apparently impenetrable wall of leaves in front of him, and said softly:

"How do I get through?"

"Burrow, of course," whispered the voice impatiently.

He obeyed, and stooping a little plunged his head and arms among the leaves and began working his way into them like a mole. When he was entirely inside the doorway he wriggled around and pulled the door shut behind him. The leaves made hardly any noise as he inched through them. There was just enough air to breathe, and a dryish aromatic scent. His progress was slow, and it seemed to take about ten minutes before the leaves began to thin out, and striking upward like a diver he finally came to the surface.

He was in a room, or so he supposed, having come into it through an ordinary door in a corridor, but the walls could not be seen at all on account of the rampart of leaves piled up all round him. Toward the center there was a clear space on the ground, and in this grew a mighty trunk, as large round as a table, covered with roughish silver bark, all protrusions and knobs. The branches began above his head, thrusting out laterally like those of an oak or beech, but very little could be seen of them on account of the leaves which grew everywhere in thick clusters, and the upper reaches of the tree were not visible at all. The growing leaves were yellow—not the faded yellow of autumn but a brilliant gold which illuminated the room. At least there was no other source of light, and it was not dark.

There appeared to be no one else under the tree and Wil wondered who had spoken to him and where they could be.

As if in answer to his thoughts the voice spoke again: "Can't you climb up?"

"Yes, of course I can," he said, annoyed with himself for not thinking of this, and he began setting his feet on the rough ledges of bark and pulling himself up. Soon he could not see the floor below, and was in a cage of leaves which fluttered all round him, dazzling his eyes. The scent in the tree was like thyme on the downs on a hot summer's day.

"Where are you?" he asked in bewilderment.

He heard a giggle.

"I'm here," said the voice, and he saw an agitation among the leaves at the end of a branch, and worked his way out to it. He found a little girl—a rather plain little girl with freckles and reddish hair hidden under some kind of cap. She wore a long green velvet dress and a ruff, and she was seated comfortably swinging herself up and down in a natural hammock of small branches.

"Really I thought you'd *never* find your way here," she said, giving him a derisive welcoming grin.

"I'm not used to climbing trees," he excused himself.

"I know, poor wretch. Never mind, this one's easy enough. What's your name? Mine's Em."

"Mine's Wil. Do you live here?"

"Of course. This isn't really my branch—some of them are very severe about staying on their own branches—look at *him.*" She indicated a very Puritanical-looking gentleman in black knee-breeches who appeared for a moment and then vanished again as a cluster of leaves swayed. "*I* go where I like, though. My branch isn't respectable—we were on the wrong side in every war from Matilda and Stephen on. As soon as the colonies were invented they shipped a lot of us out there, but it was no use, they left a lot behind. They always hope that we'll die out, but of course we don't. Shall I show you some of the tree?"

"Yes, please."

"Come along then. Don't be frightened, you can hold my hand a lot of the time. It's almost as easy as stairs."

When she began leading him about he realized that the

tree was much more enormous than he had supposed; in fact he did not understand how it could be growing in a room inside a house. The branches curved about making platforms, caves, spiral staircases, seats, cupboards and cages. Em led him through the maze, which she seemed to know by heart, pushing past the clusters of yellow leaves. She showed him how to swing from one branch to another, how to slide down the slopes and wriggle through the crevices, and how to lie back in a network of boughs and rest his head on a thick pillow of leaves.

They made quite a lot of noise and several disapproving old faces peered at them from the ends of branches, though one crusader smiled faintly and his dog wagged its tail.

"Have you anything to eat?" asked Em presently, mopping her brow with her kerchief.

"Yes, I've got some biscuits I didn't eat at break this morning. I'm not allowed to keep them of course, they'd be cross if they knew."

"Of course," nodded Em, taking a biscuit. "Thanks. Dryish, your comfits, aren't they—but welcome. Wait a minute and I'll bring you a drink." She disappeared among the boughs and came back in a few moments with two little greenish crystal cups full of a golden liquid.

"It's sap," she said, passing one over. "It has a sort of forest taste, hasn't it; makes you think of horns. Now I'll give you a present."

She took the cups away and he heard her rummaging somewhere down by the trunk of the tree.

"There's all sorts of odds and ends down there. This is the first thing I could find. Do you like it?"

"Yes, very much," he said, handling the slender silver thing with interest. "What is it?"

She looked at it critically. "I think it's the shoehorn that Queen Elizabeth used (she always had trouble with wearing too tight shoes). She must have left it behind here sometime. You can have it anyway—you might find a use for it. You'd better be going now or you'll be in trouble and then it won't be so easy for you to come here another time."

"How shall I ever find my way back here?"

"You must stand quite still and listen. You'll hear me whisper, and the leaves rustling. Good-bye." She suddenly put a skinny little arm round his neck and gave him a hug. "It's nice having someone to play with; I've been a bit bored sometimes."

Wil squirmed out through the leaves again and shut the door, turning to look at it as he did so. There was nothing in the least unusual about its appearance.

When he arrived back in the schoolroom (after some false turnings) he found his Aunt Agatha waiting for him. Squabb and Buckle were hovering on the threshold, but she dismissed them with a wave of her hand. The occasion was too serious for underlings.

"Wilfred," she said, in a very awful tone.

"Yes, Aunt Agatha."

"Where have you been?"

"Playing in the back part of the house."

"*Playing!* A child of your standing and responsibilities playing? Instead of getting on with your transfers? What is that?" She pounced on him and dragged out the shoehorn which was protruding from his pocket.

"Concealment! I suppose you found this and intended to creep out and sell it to some museum. You are an exceedingly wicked, disobedient boy, and as punishment for running away and hiding in this manner you will go to bed as soon as I have finished with you, you will have nothing to eat but toast-gruel, and you will have to take off your clothes *yourself,* and feed *yourself,* like a common child."

"Yes, Aunt."

"You know that you are the Heir to this noble house (when your great-uncle Winthrop dies)?"

"Yes, Aunt."

"Do you know anything about your parents?"

"No."

"It is as well. Look at this." She pulled out a little case, containing two miniatures of perfectly ordinary people. Wil studied them.

"That is your father—our brother. He disgraced the family—he sullied the scutcheon—by becoming—*a writer,* and worse—he married a *female writer,* your mother. Mercifully for the family reputation they were both drowned in the *Oranjeboot* disaster, before anything worse could happen. You were rescued, floating in a pickle barrel. *Now* do you see why we all take such pains with your education? It is to save you from the taint of your unfortunate parentage."

Wil was still digesting this when there came a knock at the door and Mr. Buckle put his head round.

"There is a Mr. Slockenheimer demanding to see you, Lady Agatha," he said. "Apparently he will not take No for an answer. Shall I continue with the reprimand?"

"No, Buckle—you presume," said Aunt Agatha coldly. "I have finished."

Wil put himself to bed, watched minutely by Buckle to see that he did not omit to brush his teeth with the silver brush or comb his eyebrows with King Alfred's comb in the manner befitting an heir of Troy. The toast and water was brought in a gold porringer. Wil ate it absently; it was very nasty, but he was so overcome by the luck of not having been found out, and wondering how he could get back to see Em another time, that he hardly noticed it.

Next morning at breakfast (which he had with his relatives) he expected to be in disgrace, but curiously enough they paid no attention to him. They were all talking about Mr. Slockenheimer.

"Such a piece of luck," said Cousin Cedric. "Just as the tourist season is ending."

"Who is this man?" creaked Great-Aunt Gertrude.

"He is a film director, from Hollywood," explained Aunt Agatha, loudly and patiently. "He is making a film about Robin Hood and he has asked permission to shoot some of the indoor scenes in Troy—for which we shall all be handsomely paid, naturally."

"Naturally, naturally," croaked the old ravens, all round the table.

Wil pricked up his ears, and then an anxious thought struck him. Supposing Mr. Slockenheimer's people discovered the room with the tree?

"They are coming today," Uncle Umbert was shrieking into Great-Uncle Ulric's ear trumpet.

Mr. Slockenheimer's outfit arrived after breakfast while Wil was doing his daily run—a hundred times round the triangle of grass in front of the house, while Mr. Buckle timed him with a stop watch.

A lovely lady shot out of a huge green motor car, shrieked:

"Oh, you cute darling! Now you must tell me the way to the nearest milk bar," and whisked him back into the car with her. Out of the corner of his eye he saw that Mr.

Buckle had been commandeered to show somebody the spiral staircase.

Wil ate his raspberry sundae in a daze. He had never been in the milk bar before, never eaten ice cream, never ridden in a car. To have it all following on his discovery of the day before was almost too much for him.

"Gracious!" exclaimed his new friend, looking at her wristwatch. "I must be on the set! I'm Maid Marian, you know. Tarzan, I mean Robin, has to rescue me from the wicked baron at eleven in the Great Hall."

"I'll show you where it is," said Wil.

He expected more trouble when he reached home, but the whole household was disorganized; Mr. Buckle was showing Robin Hood how to put on the Black Prince's casque (which was too big) and Aunt Agatha was having a long business conversation with Mr. Slockenheimer, so his arrival passed unnoticed.

He was relieved to find that the film was only going to be shot in the main public rooms, so there did not seem to be much risk of the tree being discovered.

After lunch Mr. Buckle was called on again to demonstrate the firing of the ninth Earl's crossbow (he shot an extra) and Wil was able to escape once more and reach in safety the regions at the back.

He stood on a dark landing for what seemed like hours, listening to the patter of his own heart. Then, tickling his ear like a thread of cobweb he heard Em's whisper:

"Wil! Here I am! This way!" and below it he heard the rustle of the tree, as if it, too, were whispering: "Here I am."

It did not take him long to find the room, but his progress through the leaves was slightly impeded by the things he was carrying. When he emerged at the foot of the tree he found Em waiting there. The hug she gave him nearly throttled him.

"I've been thinking of some more places to show you. And all sorts of games to play!"

"I've brought you a present," he said, emptying his pockets.

"Oh! What's in those little tubs?"

"Ice cream. The chief electrician gave them to me."

"What a strange confection," she said, tasting it. "It is smooth and sweet but it makes my teeth chatter."

"And here's your present." It was a gold Mickey Mouse with ruby eyes which Maid Marian had given him. Em handled it with respect and presently stored it away in one of her hidey holes in the trunk. Then they played follow-my-leader until they were so tired that they had to lie back on thick beds of leaves and rest.

"I did not expect to see you again so soon," said Em as they lay picking the aromatic leaves and chewing them, while a prim Jacobean lady shook her head at them.

Wil explained about the invasion of the film company and she listened with interest.

"A sort of strolling players," she commented. "My father was one—flat contrary to the family's commands, of course. I saw many pieces performed before I was rescued from the life by my respected grandmother to be brought up as befitted one of our name." She sighed.

For the next two months Wil found many opportunities to slip off and visit Em, for Mr. Buckle became greatly in demand as an adviser on matters of costume, and even Squabb was pressed into service ironing doublets and mending hose.

But one day Wil saw his relatives at breakfast with

long faces, and he learned that the company had finished shooting the inside scenes and were about to move to Florida to take the Sherwood Forest sequences. The handsome additional income which the family had been making was about to cease, and Wil realized with dismay that the old life would begin again.

Later when he was starting off to visit Em he found a little group, consisting of Aunt Agatha, Uncle Umbert, Mr. Slockenheimer, and his secretary, Mr. Jakes, on one of the back landings. Wil shrank into the shadows and listened to their conversation with alarm.

"One million," Mr. Slockenheimer was saying. "Yes, sir, one million's my last word. But I'll ship the house over to Hollywood myself, as carefully as if it was a new-laid egg. You may be sure of that, ma'am, I appreciate your feelings, and you and all your family may go on living in it for the rest of your days. Every brick will be numbered and every floorboard will be lettered so that they'll go back in their exact places. This house certainly will be a gold mine to me—it'll save its value twice over in a year as sets for different films. There's Tudor, Gothic, Norman, Saxon, Georgian, Decorated, all under one roof."

"But we shall have to have salaries, too, mind," said Uncle Umbert greedily. "We can't be expected to uproot ourselves like this and move to Hollywood all for nothing."

Mr. Slockenheimer raised his eyebrows at this, but said agreeably:

"Okay, I'll sign you on as extras." He pulled out a fistful of forms, scribbled his signature on them, and handed them to Aunt Agatha. "There you are, ma'am, twenty-year contracts for the whole bunch."

"Dirt cheap at the price, even so," Wil heard him whisper to the secretary.

"Now as we've finished shooting I'll have the masons in tomorrow and start chipping the old place to bits. Hangings and furniture will be crated separately. It'll take quite a time, of course; shouldn't think we'll get it done under three weeks." He looked with respect over his shoulder at a vista of dark corridor which stretched away for half a mile.

Wil stole away with his heart thudding. Were they actually proposing to pull down the house, *this* house, and ship it to Hollywood for film sets? What about the tree? Would they hack it down, or dig it up and transport it, leaves and all?

"What's the matter, boy?" asked Em, her cheek bulging with the giant humbug he had brought her.

"The film company's moving away; and they're going to take Troy with them for using as backgrounds for films."

"The whole house?"

"Yes."

"Oh," said Em, and became very thoughtful.

"Em."

"Yes?"

"What—I mean, what would happen to you if they found this room and cut the tree down, or dug it up?"

"I'm not sure," she said, pondering. "I shouldn't go *on* after that—none of us would in here—but as to exactly *what* would happen—; I don't expect it would be bad. Perhaps we should just go out like lamps."

"Well, then, it must be stopped," said Wil so firmly that he surprised himself.

"Can you forbid it? You're the Heir, aren't you?"

"Not till old Uncle Winthrop dies. We'll have to think of some other plan."

"I have an idea," said Em, wrinkling her brow with effort. "In my days, producers would do much for a well-written new play, one that had never been seen before. Is it still like that nowadays?"

"Yes I think so, but we don't know anyone who writes plays," Wil pointed out.

"I have a play laid by somewhere," she explained. "The writer was a friend of my father—he asked my father to take it up to London to have it printed. My father bade me take care of it and I put it in my bundle of clothes. It was on that journey, as we were passing through Oxford, that I was seen and carried off by my respected grandmother, and I never saw my father or Mr. Shakespeere again, so the poor man lost his play."

"Mr. Shakespeere, did you say?" asked Wil, stuttering slightly. "What was the name of the play?"

"I forget. I have it here somewhere." She began delving about in a cranny between two branches and presently drew out a dirty old manuscript. Wil stared at it with popping eyes.

The Tragicall Historie of Robin Hoode
A play by Wm. Shakespeere
Act 1, Scene I. Sherwood Forest. Enter John Lackland, De Bracy, Sheriff of Nottingham, Knights, Lackeys and attendants.

JOHN L. Good sirs, the occasion of our coming hither
  Is, since our worthy brother Coeur de Lion
  Far from our isle now wars on Paynim soil,
  The apprehension of that recreant knave
  Most caitiff outlaw who is known by some

As Robin Locksley; by others Robin Hood;
More, since our coffers gape with idle locks
The forfeiture of his ill-gotten gains.
Thus Locksley's stocks will stock our locks
    enow
While he treads air beneath the forest bough.

"Golly," said Wil. "Shakespeere's *Robin Hood.* I wonder what Mr. Slockenheimer would say to this?"

"Well don't wait. *Go and ask him.* It's yours—I'll make you a present of it."

He wriggled back through the leaves with frantic speed, slammed the door, and raced down the passage toward the Great Hall. Mr. Slockenheimer was there superintending the packing of some expensive and elaborate apparatus.

"Hello, Junior. Haven't seen you in days. Well, how d'you like the thought of moving to Hollywood, eh?"

"Not very much," said Wil frankly. "You see, I'm used to it here, and—and the house is too; I don't think the move would be good for it."

"Think the dry air would crumble it, mebbe? Well, there's something to what you say. I'll put in air-conditioning apparatus the other end. I'm sorry you don't take to the idea, though. Hollywood's a swell place."

"Mr. Slockenheimer," said Wil. "I've got something here which is rather valuable. It's mine—somebody gave it to me. And it's genuine. I was wondering if I could do a sort of swap—exchange it for the house, you know."

"It would have to be mighty valuable," replied Mr. Slockenheimer cautiously. "Think it's worth a million, son? What is it?"

"It's a play by Mr. Shakespeere—a new play that no one's seen before."

"Eh?"

"I'll show you," said Wil confidently, pulling out the MS.

"The Tragicall Historie of Robin Hoode," read Mr. Slockenheimer slowly. "By Wm. Shakespeere. Well, I'll be gosh darned. Just when I'd finished the indoor scenes. Isn't that just my luck. Hey, Junior—are you sure this is genuine?—Well, Jakes will know, he knows everything; hey," he called to his secretary, "come and have a look at this."

The dry Mr. Jakes let out a whistle when he saw the signature.

"That's genuine all right," he said. "It's quite something you've got there. First production of the original Shakespeare play by Q. P. Slockenheimer."

"Well, will you swap?" asked Wil once more.

"I'll say I will," exclaimed Mr. Slockenheimer slapping him thunderously on the back. "You can keep your moldering old barracks. I'll send you twenty stalls for the premiere. *Robin Hoode by Wm. Shakespeere.* Well, what do you know!"

"There's just one thing," said Wil pausing.

"Yes, Bud?"

"These contracts you gave my uncle and aunt and the others. Are they still binding?"

"Not if you don't want."

"Oh, but I do—I'd much rather they went to Hollywood."

Mr. Slockenheimer burst out laughing.

"Oh, I get the drift. Okay, Junior, I daresay they won't bother me as much as they do you. I'll hold them to those contracts as tight as glue. Twenty years, eh? You'll be of age by then, I guess? Your Uncle Umbert can be the Sheriff of Nottingham, he's about the build for the part. And we'll fit your Aunt Aggie in somewhere."

"And Buckle and Squabb?"

"Yes, yes," said Mr. Slockenheimer, much tickled. "Though what you'll do here all on your own—however, that's your affair. Right, boys, pack up those cameras next."

Three days later the whole outfit was gone, and with them, swept away among the flash bulbs, cameras, extras, crates, props and costumes, went Squabb, Buckle, Aunt Agatha, Uncle Umbert, Cousin Cedric, and all the rest.

Empty and peaceful the old house dreamed, with sunlight shifting from room to room and no sound to break the silence, save in one place, where the voices of children could be heard faintly above the rustling of a tree.

Howard M. Fast,
"The Brood"

In 1872 Jim is "thirteen, tall, gangling, skinny, ugly."
His family of eight is heading westward, the Rocky
Mountains in sight, but as the story opens their world is
not one of movement or wide-open prairies or approaching mountain ranges. Instead, that world is defined by
eighteen wagons pulled into a defensive circle around a
shelter pit, a dwindling water supply, and the graves of
three men killed in the Indians' first attack. Jim's place
within that circle is not clear to him. Too young to join
the men, armed and ready beneath the wagons, he still
finds himself locked in childish squabbling with the five
other children and proud though misplaced defiance of
his mother. Within this starkly defined area Jim begins to
understand his parents better and is confronted with a
clear role.

The Brood
by Howard M. Fast

HE WOKE, LOOKED into the hot sun, then closed his eyes and sought the dark restfulness of sleep. But the sun burned through his lids; awake, he heard a thousand noises that were not there before. He gave up sleep, and came alive as he always came alive at the beginning of a day. He came alive not as himself, but as the oldest of the brood. As himself, he had almost no identity; as one of the brood, he was one of six scrambling, squabbling, jealous bits of life.

As himself, he was a boy of thirteen, tall, gangling, skinny, ugly. A bony, sheepish face; bony hands that did the wrong thing instinctively, that invited blame.

As of the brood, he was Jim, the oldest. His sister, Jenny, was a year younger; his brother, Ben, nine; his brother, Cal, eight; his sister, Lizzie, six; the baby, Peter, was fifteen months, stub of the brood.

He, Jim, became awake—to sound, to light, to consciousness of time and distance. Time and distance stretched out, and always eighteen sway-backed covered wagons were his world. In that world he lived, fought, bickered, slept, and waked. Past and future were as nothing; for only intermittently did he think of the place where they had originated, and hardly at all of the vague place to which they were going. That it was the year eighteen seventy-two meant little to him; that the purple haze on the western horizon was the hump of the continent, the Rocky Mountains, meant even less. The world was within the circle of wagons, and that was all the world.

Becoming awake that way, to heat, to smells of cooking, he felt the contact of his sister Jenny's ribs pressing his elbow. He jabbed with his elbow, felt his sister twitch out of sleep, jabbed again, and heard her offended cry.

"You lemme alone!" she screamed.

He sat up, a smirk on his long, sun-splotched face, his lips pursed and whistling: "Oh! Susanna, oh, don't you cry for me—"

Jenny kicked out. He rolled her over, went on with his whistling. He became aware of his mother's approach, a big woman, large of bone, of hand and foot. She carried the baby, and she walked strangely, bent almost double. There was a reason for the crouched walk, and for a moment it drove all else from Jim's mind, leaving only the world he knew, the world of eighteen wagons that had moved constantly westward, but now moved no longer; the world that had thrown itself into a circle, a wall of wagons, a shelter pit in the center, an enemy outside. Jim thought of the enemy, the brown enemy, the painted enemy, of arrows that quivered loosely in sandy soil. Thoughts of the enemy mingled with plans and devices for outwitting his sister. He forgot the enemy and continued his whistling.

"Maw, he's hittin' me again."

He whistled calmly.

"Stop that whistling!" his mother ordered. She put down the baby. It was early morning, but already her face showed lines of weariness.

"He hit me," Jenny said.

"She's a liar." The words came out instinctively, with a rush, and his face assumed the sheepish look that was a confession. They would all be against him. If he hadn't hit her, she would have plagued him until he had. Regardless of what he did or didn't do, it was wrong. The oldest of the brood, he was bound by it. His lanky, awkward body incurred their derision, not their respect. In that moment he hated them.

"Jim! Jim, don't you call nobody a liar, or I'll lick the livin' daylights outta you." His mother sighed, sank to the ground. She was a tall woman, too tall for the shelter pit. All day under the hot sun she had to crouch and hide the length of her body.

"Maw, look, he hit me here."

Other bits of the brood had come to life. "I seen him," Ben said, joining in the argument.

"Stop that whistling!" She slapped him.

He kicked out of the blankets and stalked off. Clothed; but barefoot, he had slept. He took pleasure in the fact that he wouldn't be ordered to wash, to dress. The slap still stung, and he made up his mind that Ben would feel the weight of his own hand.

"Bend your head!" his mother ordered.

His sister Jenny was laughing.

He stood defiantly erect. That way, erect, he stood too high. His head rose above the edge of the scooped hole that housed their world, that had been their world for two days now. His head was high enough for him to see beyond the boundary of fresh-piled dirt, for him to see the eighteen long canvas-covered wagons, drawn into a circle and chained wheel to wheel, for him to see the men who lay under the wagons, between the wheels, guns held.

"Jim, you—get your head down!" his mother cried.

Jenny made a face. "Too tall for his own good, ain' he, Maw?"

"Jim, you come back here!"

He stood wavering, shamefaced, hot about his ears, conscious of smiling glances from many other families in the pit, hating the brood he was a part of.

"Jim!"

He shuffled back. The hot, fresh-turned dirt of the pit broke between his toes. He came back to the brood with his head bent. Jenny made faces. Lizzie grinned at him with impish satisfaction.

"Never seen a boy like you," his mother sighed. "Never seen a boy to make his mother's life a trial."

"What I done?" he demanded.

Jenny cried: "He don' know, Maw. Jus' listen, he don' know."

"Shut up!" Jim cried.

His mother's hand stung on his face. She thrust a pail at him. "See you don't spill the water," she told him.

Pail in hand, he started across the shelter pit. He kept his head erect, defiantly, glancing eagerly at the linked wagons, at the sweat-soaked men who lay beneath them, rifles in hand, at the sweep of yellow, sun-dried prairie beyond, at the hazy mystery of the landscape where the enemy waited. He indulged in generous self-pity, seeing himself there with the men, wounded, herolike.

His mother's voice came after him, "You, Jim—get your head down!"

Close to the center of the shelter pit, sunk into the earth and covered with canvas, was all that remained of the water, some eight barrels. Other boys were there waiting, pails in hand, ill-at-ease members of broods, conscious of a gawky, adolescent uselessness; more vaguely conscious that they were sent here because their mothers feared to face the diminishing water supply.

Mr. Johnson, one arm in a sling, his long mustache drooping and sorrowful, dispensed the water. He dipped it out of a barrel with a quart dipper, allowing a quart a day for each member of each family. It was little enough, yet too much, and his hand shook like a miser's as he poured the water. A thousand times he had counted the quarts of water in camp.

The boys crowded around him, asking questions, jostling one another, able to stand erect because here the pit was deeper, but trying to give the impression that they would have stood erect anyway.

"Expect attack soon, Jack?"

"Reckon that wound hurts?"

He poured the water carefully, gently.

"How about a little drink, Jack?"

He looked down his mustache with scorn, poured the water.

"How about the cavalry, Jack? How come they ain' here?"

"How come you all talk so much?" he demanded.

Jim's turn came. "Seven," he said. He tried to look important. That was a big family; not many families could demand seven quarts of water.

Johnson poured the seven quarts.

"My, it looks cold," Jim said. "My, I'd like to have one little drink."

"You'd cheat on the water," Johnson said shortly.

Jim flung a hand at the men beneath the wagons. "Them out there—they got plenty drinkin'."

"Maybe you'd like to be out there?"

"Maybe I would."

Johnson spat his contempt, and Jim felt the red burn about his ears. He turned and started back, holding the heavy pail with both hands.

Johnson called after him, "Mind that water gets to your maw!"

The boys laughing, Johnson's mournful mustache hiding his contempt, the hot sun, the dust, the close contact of eighteen families in the narrow boundaries of the pit, his sister Jenny running toward him, warning shrilly that water was slopping over the edge of the bucket, dancing around him—

"Leggo my hand!" he cried.

His mother: "Jim—be careful!"

Then he fell, and the water swirled out into a loose splotch of brown mud, over himself, over his sister. He rose awkwardly, red hot, bitter, conscious that every eye in the pit was upon him. He picked up the empty pail and looked into it. He raised his eyes and saw his mother approaching him.

There were no words he could say. He stood stockstill, holding the bucket, until he felt the bulk of his mother's presence.

She said slowly, "Seven quarts of water—"

Every eye in the shelter pit was upon him, yet he felt alone in an immensity of sun-baked prairie, unprotected, too big for himself, all hands and feet and flushed neck.

"A day's water," his mother said.

"I'll go back. Maybe Mr. Johnson—"

"You won't go back. We'll do without."

He looked up at his mother, choked in his throat and his chest, wanting to cry, yet unable to cry. Then he turned and walked across the pit. Eyes followed him; no words, but turning eyes all the short way, past Johnson and the water barrels, past three graves with wooden crosses over them, past seven wounded men, who lay under a bit of canvas.

For a long time he sat with his back against the loose-dirt side of the pit, his knees drawn up, hands about them, bare feet plucking at the ground, the sun burning down and turning his neck a brighter red. The life of the pit went on and ignored him. The sun beat down. Breakfast was cooked and eaten. Water was hoarded and sipped. His lips became dry and cracked, his throat tight and sore. He longed for anything to happen, for attack, for rescue, for obliteration. His self-pity grew and swelled. His hatred for the brood increased.

At last he saw his mother coming toward him, bent over as she walked, carrying a plate of beans and a cup of water. She came up to him and held out the water.

"I ain' thirsty," he said.

"Drink it." Her voice was almost gentle.

He pursed up his lips and began to whistle: "Oh! Susanna, oh, don't you cry for me—"

She opened her mouth, as if to say something, as if to lash him with the usual torrent of words, then left the words unspoken, stared at him as if she were seeing him for the first time, seeing something beyond the bony awkwardness of him. There was something like satisfied relief in her eyes.

She nodded, then placed the cup of water and the plate of beans on the ground beside him. As she walked away, his dry, broken whistling followed her: "I've come from Alabama with my banjo on my knee—"

Slow time and slow passage of the sun overhead. The

heavy juice of the beans dried out, and their skins cracked. The water in the cup became cloudy with dust. The animation of the pit disappeared. Women and children were waiting. For two days now they had crouched behind their wall of wagons, waiting. One quick, furious attack had left seven wounded and three dead. Since then they had waited—for attack, for rescue, for hope, for death. The sun swung, as on a tight-drawn rubber band.

He was very hungry, even more thirsty. Again and again, he looked down at the beans and water. He whistled until his lips were too dry for the sound to emerge, and then he sat with his cracked lips drawn tight.

The sun hung above them, then started its long sway to the other side of the world. Tiny shadows lengthened. Exhausted, parched, the people of the pit lay still. Only the wounded moaned sometimes, and sometimes those who had their dead wept for them.

His brother Ben crept across to him once. Jim ignored him.

"Spilled seven quart water," Ben said.

Jim pursed his lips to whistle.

"Seven quart."

"You git," Jim whispered, his voice hoarse with hate.

"Seven quart." Ben grinned. Then he crept away.

Tiny swarming flies settled on the beans. Ants fought for their share. Jim felt the painful kneading of his stomach.

The shadows were longer when he picked up the cup of water, held it carefully, and slipped over the edge of the rifle pit. He crawled slowly, balancing the water, moving between staked horses and oxen. That way, he made a circuit of six or seven wagons before he saw his father.

Before, always before, his father had been of the brood, part of the brood, a man whose heavy-skinned hands changed slowly from a tight grasp of plow handles, to ax handles, to rake handles, a tired man sitting at a table and eating great quantities of food, not a man for love or violent passions. He had pictures of his father that went far back; but always the pictures were the same—a middle-size man plodding behind a plow, a middle-size man harnessing horses. In the same way that he resented his brothers and sisters, he had resented his father, as if he recognized his father's disappointment in his first-born. His father was a man of few words; but often, very often, Jim had felt his heavy hand on head or body.

So now he puzzled, wondered at himself, carrying a cup of water to his father.

And this father was different, a father braced against a wagon wheel, with a rifle thrust through the spokes. A motionless father, lying in the wagon's shadow.

With the cup of water held in front of him, Jim watched his father, the water so close to his nose that he could smell the warm, soured odor of it. He watched his father, seeking movement, seeking signs that would explain the vague relationship he held to this man, origin of the brood, reasons for their westward passage, reasons for the alien, hateful bits of flesh that were his brothers and sisters.

The sun was hot, but so immersed was he in the new manifestation of his father that he forgot the sun's heat, that he forgot his thirst and hunger, that he forgot his hate and resentment of the world about him. Slowly he was discovering ties that bound him to the man, was reaching back for them.

He watched his father's movement, watched an arm

stretch, saw a leg ease itself from a cramped position, saw a ripple of undulation travel through the whole body. The other men talked occasionally, in short, terse sentences; but his father lay there in silence.

He wanted to crawl forward toward his father, yet something held him back, the same thing that kept him wordless when his mother came with water and beans. For the first time in all his life he felt a sudden, awful pity for his father, for his mother.

Then he saw it, far out on the prairie—dust and through the dust men emerging. And he knew instinctively what it was, what the two days of waiting had been for. Not moving, not afraid, clutching the cup of water in his hand, he lay there and watched the line of dark men on small horses charge the circled wagons. He watched them come out of the dust like bathers breaking from the surf, heard their shrill screams, and saw them break against the rifle fire as against a solid wall.

After that, the fight might have been hours or minutes. He didn't know—as if his life had been suspended for that time, to be resumed again. He saw the changing positions of his father's body as he aimed and fired, and he felt with his father for the brood that lay in the shelter pit—fear, anxiety. He aimed with his father, fired with the toil-hardened hands, saw the dark riders come to the edge of the wagons again and again, beaten back on their rearing horses, screaming, charging, racing along the wagons, hurling slim lances. Bullets kicked sand into his face, and once an arrow sank quivering into the ground beside him, within an inch of his elbow.

He saw his father struck, saw the arrow quivering up from between his neck and shoulder, felt the rending, hot pain of it, as if it had been in his own flesh.

He crawled forward, still holding the cup of water. The water was dirty and yellow. Sand lay on the bottom of the cup. Dust made a film over the water.

His father had rolled over; lay on his back. Jim's bare foot came in contact with the rifle barrel, and he felt the heat of it. It came as a surprise to him that he should be able to feel anything like that now.

His father looked at him, wide, hurt, surprised eyes. "You—Jim," he managed to say, "how come you're out here?"

Even now, knowing that death had taken hold of the man, sensing the thousand things left unsaid that should have been said, Jim was unable to bridge the gap with words. "I brung you some water."

"Out here—it ain' fit for you to be out here."

Strangely, he had no desire to cry; he knew he would never cry again. "I reckoned you'd be thirsty," Jim said.

"Thirsty?"

"A little water to drink," Jim said.

He put down the water, carefully, in his mind a picture of the seven quarts he had spilled that morning. He got an arm under his father's shoulders, and with an effort, raised him a little. He saw the pain cross his father's face.

"Hurts?"

"Maybe a mite, Jim." He twisted his head, so as to look beyond the wagons, and saw that the fight was over, that the lean riders had gone, leaving behind them a few riderless horses, a few dark, twisted bodies. "Maybe a mite, Jim," he repeated.

"I brung some water."

Pain again. "I could stand a little drink of water, Jim."

He held the cup to his father's lips, feeling the stubble

of beard against his fingers, an intimacy strange and wonderful.

"That water tastes good, Jim."

"Drink it all."

"A mite more—cold inside."

"You'll be all right, Pa."

"Don't go worryin', Jim."

"I ain' worryin', Pa."

"A little more water—"

The cup was empty. Jim looked down at his father's face, at the hard lines, at the open eyes that saw nothing. He touched his father's face, the curling hairs of his beard, the dry lips.

"Jim."

He raised his eyes and saw men standing over him, wondered vaguely how long they had been there, felt resentment at their presence—almost as if they were intruding.

"Jim, better come along."

He shook his head. More than anything, he felt that he must stay there beside his father.

"Come along, Jim."

"I'll stay here. You get Maw."

Their eyes held his. He rose slowly, shaking his head, and old Captain Brady took his arm and guided him along.

His mother lay outside the shelter pit, and a blanket covered her. They drew back the blanket, so he could see her face. Her face was peaceful, not like his father's, but with closed eyes, with some of the lines erased from the skin. The lips were not hard, and he tried to remember if they had ever been hard. He wanted to touch the lips, just to lay the tips of his fingers against them. They were cold; the rush of fear was like ice over his body. He wasn't afraid because she was dead; he was afraid because he understood for the first time how it was with them, with the brood, because he knew instinctively with what passion they were conceived, with what suffering.

"She come outta the pit after me," Jim muttered.

"There ain' no use cryin', Jim," Captain Brady told him.

Vaguely conscious that they were there—his sister Jenny, his brother Ben, Cal, Lizzie—all the brood, all the bits of flesh from the same tree, jealous, squabbling, he said, "I ain' cryin'," his voice hoarse and too old for him. He pointed to his brothers and sisters. "Get outta here."

Evening almost by now, and long shadows from the wagons, and a wind out of the sunburnt stretches of the plains.

He saw the brood staring at him, wondering. Then he saw them stumbling away, Jenny crying, Ben frightened, Cal glancing back at his mother's still face.

"No use stayin' here, Jim," Captain Brady said gently. "You gotta take things like a man, Jim. That's how it is. All this—well, maybe none of us reckoned on all this. We set out to make new homes somewhere, and that's about all we thought of. I guess none of us reckoned on this. But it come, an' that's all. When somethin' comes, you take it, else it crumples you up."

"She come outta the pit after me," Jim mumbled. "She knowed I was out here, so she come after me. Seven quart a water I spilled this morn. And still she got me a cup a water somehow." He took a deep breath, remembering his father. "I went to take him a cup a water. I got to thinkin' there wasn't one thing all my life I done for him that way, like takin' him a cup a water to drink out of.

All my life long, not one thing. And then I took the water to bring along to him, an' right there I couldn't give it to him. Maybe I was afraid he'd lick me for comin' outta the pit—"

"Mind me now, Jim," Captain Brady said. "They're sleepin' peaceful-like, an' can't harm or trouble come to them anymore. But we got to move on. We're low on water an' low on food. Maybe they'll attack again an' maybe they won't, but we got to move on. They had enough to last them now till morn, I reckon. It's forty mile to Fort Smith, an' we reckon to travel all night. Maybe we'll hit it by dawn, maybe not; but we'll push on. You got to think about that. We're set to split you up, you an' your brothers an' sisters, maybe one or two to a wagon—"

"We got a wagon," Jim said.

"All right, Jim. But it's a long way West."

"Not so long now."

"If you're gonna act pigheaded, Jim—"

"Maybe I am. You ain't splittin' us up, Captain. We gotta wagon, an' got horses. We'll get along."

"What about the baby?"

"I guess Jenny'll mind the baby."

"Jim, you poor little damn fool, you're just a kid. You—"

"Maybe so. She come outta the pit to get me, an' she was shot. But she come outta the pit to get me."

"You poor little damn fool."

"You ain' splittin' us up."

"You poor little damn fool. Go harness up your horses."

It was dark when the eighteen wagons moved away from the shelter pit. Jim was sixth in line, holding reins to four horses. He was tall, sun-splotched, ugly, and awkward even in the dark. He sat there conscious of the brood in the wagon behind him, five bits of frightened, jealous life.

As he stirred the horses, he tried to separate himself from grief, from fear, from all fear of the future, from everything but the brood that was his and part of him. He pursed his lips and whistled: "Oh! Susanna, oh, don't you cry for me—"